If anything happened to Seth, Kim would never forgive herself.

Kim rushed forward and pushed through the cluster of people who had gathered around the scene. She made it to his side and fell on her knees next to him, resisting the strong urge to take his hand in hers; she was almost afraid to touch him.

Just then, Seth turned his head and looked at her, his beautiful sky-blue gaze hitting her like a laser. Her heart sped up as they stared at one another for one beat, then two.

His eyes widened slightly, and it looked as if he recognized her. A shaky ghost of a smile crossed his face and, strangely, Kim felt an odd yet unmistakable connection flare between them.

"Seth…" she whispered.

"Did I die?" he asked, his deep voice raspy.

Relief flooded through her. He was talking that had to be a good sign. She shook her head and grasped his icy hand, feeling tears burn her eyelids. "No, you saved both of us."

LISSA MANLEY

decided she wanted to be a published author at the ripe old age of twelve. After she read her first romance as a teenager when a neighbor gave her a box of old books, she quickly decided romance was her favorite genre, although she still enjoys digging in to a good medical thriller.

When her youngest was still in diapers, Lissa needed a break from strollers and runny noses, so she sat down and started crafting a romance, and she has been writing ever since. Nine years later she sold her first book, fulfilling her childhood dream. She feels blessed to be able to write what she loves, and intends to be writing until her fingers quit working, or she runs out of heartwarming stories to tell. She's betting the fingers will go first.

Lissa lives in the beautiful city of Portland, Oregon, with her wonderful husband of twenty-seven years, a grown daughter and college-aged son, and two bossy poodles who rule the house and get away with it. When she's not writing, she enjoys reading, crafting, bargain hunting, cooking and decorating. She loves hearing from her readers and can be reached through her website, www.lissamanley.com, or through Steeple Hill Books.

Family to the Rescue
Lissa Manley

Steeple
Hill®

Published by Steeple Hill Books™

STEEPLE HILL BOOKS

Steeple
Hill®

Recycling programs
for this product may
not exist in your area.

ISBN-13: 978-0-373-81538-8

FAMILY TO THE RESCUE

www.SteepleHill.com

Printed in U.S.A.

And without faith, it is impossible to please Him.
For whoever would draw near to God
must believe that He exists and that
He rewards those who seek Him.
—*Hebrews* 11:6

For Kevin. For always having faith in me.

Chapter One

There! A sound floated to him on the breeze. A call for help. Seth Graham was sure of it.

The hairs on his neck standing on end, he hurried to the ocean's edge, his bare feet chopping through the sand. He shaded his eyes with his hand and scanned the water, frowning. Had he imagined the thready call for help?

But then his gaze snagged on an indistinct form about thirty yards from the beach. He narrowed his eyes, trying to figure out if he was seeing a glob of kelp.

Or a person.

His best friend, Drew, ran up and stood beside him, the Frisbee they'd been throwing back and forth on the beach dangling from his fingers. "You see anything?"

Seth blinked, still staring at the shape. "I'm not sure…"

Then an arm flailed up from the dark mass and another scream sounded, more distinct this time.

That was no glob of kelp!

Seth's stomach dropped and a heart-stopping chill of dread cut through him. "Someone's out there," he said, already stripping off his T-shirt. He looked at Drew as he threw his shirt to the sand. "Call 9–1–1 and let the others know what's going on. I'm going in."

Drew didn't argue. He immediately pulled out his cell phone and started dialing, then turned and headed toward the other people from the Moonlight Cove Community Church singles group.

Seth made a break for the ocean. Just as his feet hit water, a voice called to him.

"Seth!"

He turned.

A soaking wet Lily Rogers, a former neighbor whom Seth had known for most of his twenty-eight years, came staggering down the beach toward him, her long, blond hair plastered to her head and shoulders. "The new gal, Kim, is out there," she screamed, pointing a rigid finger toward the waves. "We went in together to jump waves and got too far out. I made it in farther down, but she's caught in a riptide!"

"I'm on it!" Seth shouted, still moving. He now remembered seeing Kim—a cute brunette about his age—when he'd arrived at the cookout earlier.

Lily lurched past him and up the beach toward the bonfire spot, though she was obviously exhausted, waving her arms and yelling at the top of her lungs to alert the others to the problem.

Seth ran into the water full bore, then dove headfirst into the brine.

His breath left him in a rush as he hit the water, which was icy despite the warm July day, and he almost froze up as the ocean shocked his body. But through sheer will and physical and mental discipline honed by a few years playing pro baseball and being physically active, he managed to keep going.

About twenty yards into his rescue he stopped and lifted his head to be sure he was on the right track. Thankfully, he'd judged the direction to swim correctly. He saw the woman directly in front of him, about ten yards away, when she flung up an arm again. She hadn't sunk yet.

But she would, unless she knew what to do, which it looked like she didn't. Seth, however, had been born and raised in the coastal town of Moonlight Cove, Washington, and he knew the drill. He couldn't struggle against the rip; he had to swim parallel to the shore, not toward it.

Just as he reached the woman—Kim, Lily had said—she went under. Ignoring his own growing exhaustion, he grabbed her arm and pulled her up, noting when she surfaced that her skin was the color of snow. Her eyes fluttered. Good sign. She wasn't unconscious yet.

"Kim, I'm here to take you in," Seth told her in a firm, calm voice. "Do exactly what I say, okay?"

She nodded sluggishly.

He wrapped an arm around her narrow shoulders. "We're going to swim parallel to the shore to escape the rip, and then swim in, all right?"

Another nod, more feeble this time. She was clearly worn out. He'd arrived in the nick of time.

Seth moved his other hand beneath her arm, grasping her body in a more efficient hold. He began to swim, pulling her with him as best he could. To her credit, she made an attempt to swim with him, but she obviously didn't have any gas left, and she wasn't much help.

Neither was the riptide; he could feel the force of it swirling beneath them like a living being, pulling with a grip of steel that surprised even him. He'd always respected the power of the ocean, but this…this was unlike anything he'd ever imagined.

He sent up a prayer for the first time in ages. *God, let me be strong enough to do this.*

Focusing on moving forward with each stroke,

Seth tried not to notice how his hands and feet were growing numb. He did his best not to fight the current—that was a battle he would not win. He had to outsmart the deadly undertow.

Drawing on reserves of strength he didn't know he possessed, his movements aligned with the shore, he waited for the current to loosen its grip. His strength ebbed out of him with every moment that passed.

Seth kept swimming, hoping God would listen to a man who had a distant relationship with Him. A few long moments later, the pulling current eased a bit, but he swam about fifteen feet farther to be sure they were out of the rip—yes! Finally.

His breath burning in his lungs, his legs and arms aching with effort, he turned at a ninety degree angle and swam for shore. Which, at the moment, looked as if it were about a hundred miles away.

Was he close enough to make it?

Just as his strength was almost spent and he could barely lift his arms or kick his legs, he tentatively put his foot down to feel for the sandy bottom.

And felt sand.

Wow. For once, his prayer had been heard. And answered.

Groaning with effort, Seth put both feet down.

"Hang on to my back," he managed to shout to Kim through tight lips. "I'm gonna walk us in."

She obeyed and wrapped her ice-cold arms around his neck and hung on, piggyback style. With the last of his waning strength, he hauled her to shore.

Just as he was making headway, he stubbed his toe on a rock hidden in the surf. Pain streaked up his foot. He paused, looking for more rocks, but he couldn't see beneath the churning water. So he felt around with his other foot, hoping for safe sand.

But instead his foot encountered another rock. And another. He was surrounded. He looked to the shore and could see people congregated there, a frantic-looking Lily among them. If he could just make it a little farther...

Seth inched along, trying to avoid the rocks, his legs now completely numb. The rocks spread out a bit and gave way to more sand, and he thought he was home free, especially when he saw someone—he wasn't sure who—splash into the water, running toward them.

Thinking they'd cleared the rocks, he forced himself to move forward without feeling the terrain first with his feet. He took a step, staggered and struggled to catch himself.

All at once, out of nowhere, a bed of rocks rose in front of him as the tide swelled out. He couldn't avoid the first black and green mass and he ran his shins right into the thing. Feeling as if his legs didn't belong to him, he toppled over into the thigh-deep water like a fallen tree, Kim going with him.

As he hit the water, and what was hidden below, pain exploded in his head. And then a glacial blackness engulfed him and he knew no more.

Kim Hampton blinked her burning eyes, the taste of seawater in her mouth, her skin as cold as ice. She was surprised to see blue sky above her.

Was she in heaven?

If she was, the place looked an awful lot like earth….

An older man with a round face, curly brown hair and kind blue eyes came into her line of sight as he hovered above her. "Miss," he said. "I'm a paramedic. We're going to give you some oxygen, so just lie back and try to relax, all right?" He slowly covered her mouth and nose with the plastic apparatus he held.

Definitely not heaven.

She breathed deep and the oxygen flooded her tired lungs. Instantly, her brain cleared and reality kicked in. She felt the hard, cool sand beneath her, smelled the ocean.

Joy spread through her.

Thank You, Lord, for not making Dylan

motherless! Her precious son had already essentially lost his dad when her ex had walked out on them a year ago; at age seven, losing her would be more, she was sure, than Dylan could ever hope to deal with.

The enormity of what had almost happened to her, of what she'd almost lost, began to sink in and she started to shake.

Someone took her hand and squeezed it. Kim shifted her gaze and saw her new friend Lily seated on the sand on her other side, a fleece blanket covering her shoulders, her eyes red rimmed from crying.

"Oh, my goodness," Lily said. "I'm so glad you're all right."

Kim couldn't speak with her mouth and nose covered, so she just nodded. She was very tired. And so cold her veins felt frozen.

As if reading her thoughts, someone covered her with a soft, warm blanket. Yes, that was better.

Unbidden, memories of her harrowing time in the water flooded her mind. The brutal riptide. The cold ocean overtaking her. Her feeling of total helplessness. She'd been sure she was going to drown.

But God had heard her call for help. A man had arrived just as her body had almost been overcome with exhaustion. And he'd saved her.

Gratitude poured through her—for the man, and for the Lord.

Buoyant with relief, she removed the oxygen mask. "Where's the guy who saved me?" she asked Lily, her voice raw and trembling. "I need to see him, thank him."

Lily pressed her lips together and shook her head slightly.

Dread filled Kim. "What?" she pressed. "What happened to him?" Was he dead because of her impetuousness? She had to know what had happened, even though she'd shrivel up and die if she were responsible for another person's death.

"Seth managed the rip perfectly," Lily said.

"But?"

"But…he was completely played out when he got close to shore. He…um, fell and hit his head on a rock."

A chill from deep within spread through Kim's whole body, adding another layer of cold to her soul. "Is he all right?"

"He was unconscious very briefly, and the paramedics are working on him."

Caustic regret knifed Kim in the chest. She shouldn't have been out in those waves, shouldn't have put another person in danger. Lily had told her to be careful.

Granted, Kim was from Los Angeles, and she wasn't used to the dangerous currents that swirled around the waters of the Washington coast. Even so, she should have been smarter. More cautious.

Kim put the mask back over her nose and sucked in a huge swig of oxygen to fortify herself, then pulled the mask off. She had to see the man who'd saved her, had to know for herself how he was doing.

Could she handle it? Too bad if she couldn't. Whatever came her way was deserved; she hadn't listened to Lily. Just as she hadn't listened to the warnings not to marry Scott.

Leaping before she looked had consequences. Would she ever learn not to be so impulsive?

With shaky arms she grabbed the blanket and struggled to her feet. Her legs were rubbery and didn't want to hold her, but she forced them underneath her and stood.

Lily took hold of her elbow. "I don't think you should be up," she said. "You've been through a lot.

Lily was probably right, but Kim didn't care. She had to see her rescuer. Kim looked around, searching for the paramedic who'd been tending her.

Her gaze scanned a man lying on his back on the sand about fifteen feet away. He was surrounded by firefighters and rescue personnel—including the man who'd been taking care of her—assessing his condition.

Filled with dread, she wrapped the blanket more securely around her body and wobbled over to find out what was going on.

As she drew near, her breath snagged in her throat and she could barely breathe—maybe she should have dragged the oxygen along with her.

Her savior was a young man, maybe her age of twenty-eight—or a little older—with short dark hair and a strong, shadowed jawline. He was covered with a blanket, his face ashen, and he had a nasty cut on his forehead.

Kim felt her knees tremble, and she thought she might pass out. She gave in to her shaky legs and sank to the sand.

She pressed a hand to her knotted tummy. No, no, no.

What had she done?

Several minutes passed as the paramedics worked on Seth. Kim was stuck to the sandy beach where she sat, exhausted physically and sick at heart.

Finally, she found the strength and rose. "Is he going to be all right?" she asked the paramedics, forcing herself to move forward and face the situation rather than following her instincts and running far, far away.

One of the techs looked up from monitoring the injured man's pulse. "He's conscious now, but he's taken a pretty severe blow to the head, which can be dicey."

Dicey. That didn't sound good.

The wind kicked up, whipping Kim's blanket from around her body. A shiver ran though her as she grabbed the edges and held on to it tighter, her legs still quivering from shock and cold.

She was chilled to the bone, and not just because of the sudden gust of wind pummeling her.

Clenching her hands into fists, she stayed a ways back to let the medics work.

Lily came to her side and put a comforting arm around Kim. "Don't worry. Seth is a tough guy, and he's young and healthy." She squeezed Kim's shoulders reassuringly. "He'll pull through."

Kim hoped so with everything in her, with every fervent prayer echoing in her heart. If anything happened to this Seth, Kim would never forgive herself.

Would God? Surely He would...

Fighting back tears, she could do nothing but stand back and beg for the Lord's help from deep inside her soul.

Please, God. Help Seth pull through.

A few moments later, two burly paramedics carried a stretcher from the parking area down to the beach. Just as they put the stretcher down, Seth moved. A husky groan escaped from his blue-tinted lips and he moved his arms out from under the blanket. Kim stared at them for just a moment. Clearly the guy was in shape. No wonder he'd been able to drag her through the current.

Kim rushed forward and pushed through the cluster of singles group participants who had also gathered around the scene. She made it to his side and fell down on her knees next to him, resisting the strong urge to take his hand in hers; she was almost afraid to touch him.

Just then, he turned his head and looked at her, his beautiful sky-blue gaze hitting her like a laser. She froze, feeling his stare to the tips of her toes. Her heart sped up as they looked at one another for one beat, then two.

His eyes widened slightly, and it looked at if he recognized her. A shaky ghost of a smile crossed his face, and, strangely, Kim felt an odd yet unmistakable connection flare between them.

"Seth…" she whispered. She stretched out her hand, once again needing to touch him, comfort him, tell him how grateful she was.

"Did I die?" he asked, his deep voice raspy.

Relief flooded through her. He was talking—that had to be a good sign. She shook her head and grasped his icy hand, feeling tears burn her eyelids. "No, you saved both of us."

Before Seth could reply, one of the paramedics

touched her shoulder. "Miss, you're going to have to move out of the way. We must transport him, stat."

She nodded. Of course. Kim stood and moved back, brushing away her tears.

Shaking, she simply watched, her hands clenched together in front of her, as the techs told Seth what was happening with practiced efficiency and loaded him onto the stretcher. A tall man in a baseball cap who seemed to be part of the church group stayed by Seth's side while they carried Seth away to the ambulance waiting in the parking lot, its lights flashing.

Two paramedics stayed behind. One started cleaning up and the other approached her.

"How are you doing?" he asked Kim. "Are you feeling light-headed at all?"

Kim shook her head. "I'm okay."

"Why don't I take your blood pressure and pulse again just to be sure."

As he worked, Kim watched the paramedics load Seth into the ambulance. Lily stayed by her side, a silent support Kim appreciated.

The ambulance pulled away, and Kim watched it go with a heavy heart.

"Everything checks out normal," the paramedic said, rising. "You can go. But if you have anything come up, anything strange at all, be sure and go straight to the E.R."

Kim nodded her agreement, too numb to speak.

"Why don't you let me take you home," Lily said. "You have to be dead on your feet."

"No, I can't go home until I'm sure Seth is okay."

"I can call you when there's news—"

"No. I have to go to the hospital." Her jaw set, her mind made up, Kim stood and started walking toward where she'd left her tote bag near the bonfire spot, her tired legs having a tough time negotiating the soft sand.

Lily trotted along beside her. "Are you sure you should be driving?"

"I can handle it," Kim replied, remarkably clearheaded now that she wasn't standing around, purposeless. She might have almost drowned because of her rash decision, but she wasn't *heartless*.

Lily put a firm hand on Kim's arm. "I'll drive you in my car."

Kim was too tired to argue. She nodded as she reached her canvas bag with her stuff in it, pulled out her fleece pullover and dropped the blanket from around her shoulders. Shivering, she pulled on her sweatshirt, wondering if she'd ever be warm again. She wished she'd brought some sweatpants, too. Oh, well. Her wet board shorts would have to do. She'd put her tennis shoes on when she got to her car.

"Let's go," she said to Lily.

As they walked to the parking lot, guilt poked her.

She prayed Seth's injuries weren't too serious.

Chapter Two

Seth closed his eyes against the rhythmic pounding in his head.

Bam. Bam. Bam.

He held back a groan of pain. His head felt like he'd been hit by a Babe Ruth line drive. Five or six times.

"Would you like some pain medication?" Dr. Anderson, the older E.R. physician who'd been taking care of Seth, asked from where he stood at the end of Seth's narrow hospital bed.

"Don't need it," Seth replied. He'd been a professional athlete; he could handle pain. And after he'd watched his older brother, Curt, almost ruin his life with a prescription drug addiction, Seth hated taking any kind of medication, even aspirin.

His bushy gray eyebrows raised, Dr. Anderson looked up from Seth's chart. "Well, it's your choice, of course, but you did suffer a grade two concussion—and your laceration required ten stitches, so you're going to have some fairly significant pain."

"No drugs. No way."

"Okay. But if you change your mind…"

"I won't."

Drew poked his head around the E.R. cubicle curtain. "You ready to spring him, Doc?"

"I think so, the doctor said, looking at the clock. "I've held him for three hours, he was only unconscious briefly, he seems to have no retrograde amnesia and everything else checks out all right."

"Great," Seth said. He was anxious to leave the hospital and get home. It had been a long, hard day.

The doctor looked at Seth. "The nurse will be in with your discharge instructions."

He left and Drew entered the room. He had his baseball cap on backward, and his dark blond hair stuck out from underneath it. His brown eyes were shadowed with concern.

"How'd you get in?" Seth asked. "I thought they only allowed immediate family back here."

"Phoebe is tight with Nurse Fiona at the E.R. admission desk, so Fiona was willing to do her best friend's brother a favor," he said, clearly feeling smug.

"Ah. Always pulling strings, aren't you?"

"In important situations, yes. And this certainly qualifies." He moved farther into the curtained room and pointed to Seth's head, which was covered in a large bandage. "You're lucky you came away with only a gash on the head and a concussion." He frowned. "You could have been killed, bro."

"Nah," Seth said, waving a hand in the air, careful not to shake his aching head. "Everything would have been good if I hadn't tripped over that stupid rock."

Drew inclined his head, looking skeptical. "Maybe, maybe not. I'm just thankful you're okay." He pressed his mouth together. "I was pretty worried."

"Thanks," Seth said, deeply appreciating Drew's concern. He genuinely valued the care and compassion that came from his very limited circle of friends. "But I'm all right."

The nurse, an old battle-ax of a woman with short white hair and glasses, shoved the curtain aside and blustered in. "Mr. Graham?" she barked.

Seth winced. She was a health care professional. Couldn't she speak softly? "Yo."

She raised an eyebrow and gave him a dispassionate look. "Listen up," she said, shoving a clipboard in the air. "I have your discharge instructions."

Like a general marching into war, she reiterated what Dr. Anderson had said—that they hadn't done a CT scan because he had only been unconscious briefly, he had no retrograde amnesia in three hours of observation, and that he was to engage in no sports for a week. She added, quite succinctly, that if he had any lingering or severe symptoms, such as vomiting or onset of amnesia, he was to come back at once for a scan.

"Last but not least, Mr. Graham, you are not to be left alone for twenty-four hours," she said pointedly, glaring at him. "No exceptions."

"Excuse me?" he said.

"Standard procedure." She shrugged. "Those are the rules."

Sensing it was useless to argue, Seth took the paperwork she handed to him and signed it. He'd figure out what to do about the twenty-four-hour thing later.

His store wouldn't run itself.

Then she handed him his post-care instructions and left.

"Let's get you out of this place," Drew said. "I grabbed a T-shirt from my truck you can put on."

Seth stood and took his gown off—he still had on his board shorts from the beach—and pulled on the T-shirt Drew had brought, being careful not to touch his bandage. He looked down at his feet. "I don't suppose I came here with shoes on, did I?"

Drew shook his head. "Nope, you were barefoot, and I was so intent on staying with you, I forgot to grab your stuff. Dana Hiatt called and told me she picked up your shoes, shirt and sweatshirt when she left the beach and would drop them at your house."

"I'll have to be sure and thank her." A thought occurred to Seth. "Hey, how's Kim?" He'd been glad to see that she seemed okay when he'd come to on the beach, but you never knew.

"She's doing all right," Drew responded. "In fact, she and Lily have been camped out in the waiting room anxiously waiting for news on you."

"Hmm. I didn't expect that." Surprise tinged with pleasure bounced through Seth. For some reason, he was looking forward to seeing Kim again.

With Drew by his side, Seth made his way out of the E.R. His legs felt like he'd run a couple of marathons, and his head was pounding even more than it had when he'd been sitting.

Just as they stepped into the waiting room, a young woman rose from a chair near the exit and approached them. Her dark hair hung in damp strings around her face, and the gray fleece sweatshirt she wore was still slightly wet-looking around her shoulders. But it was her big brown eyes that stood out like hunks of topaz against the paleness of her face.

His heart sped up. *Kim.* After they'd locked gazes on the beach, he'd recognize her anywhere.

"S-Seth?" she said, her voice quavering. "I'm Kim. Kim Hampton." She tried to smile but only made her pale lips quiver. Obviously she was still shook up and exhausted.

No surprise there; he felt exactly the same way, and impersonating a banged-up piece of hamburger wasn't floating his boat.

An odd feeling twisted inside him, and a reply stuck in his throat; all he could think about was reaching out and wrapping his arms around her, giving the comfort she clearly needed.

Whoa, Graham. Slow down. Taking her in his arms? What was up with that? He barely knew her. The blow to his head must have really done a number on him.

While he stood there, wrestling with the strange urge to comfort her, she moved closer. "You rescued me today," she said, smoothing her hair behind one ear with a shaking hand. "From the water?"

"I, um, remember," he replied inanely. Oh, real smooth. When was the last time he'd sounded like an idiot while trying to talk to a woman? He guessed it was probably when he was about fifteen. He hadn't even been this tongue-tied when he had met Diana back in his rowdy college days, and he thought he'd perfected the art of casual conversation with a pretty girl since then.

"I…uh, just wanted to be sure you were okay," Kim said.

Drew cut in. "Why don't I go bring the car around while you two talk?"

"Okay," Seth said, agreeing only because he wasn't sure how far he could walk.

After Drew left, Seth looked at Kim. "I'm doing all right," he replied, even though he felt as if he had a herd of horses with sharp hooves galloping through his brain.

"Oh, good. I've been so worried." She let out a heavy breath, then eyed his bandage. "How's the cut?"

"It needed stitches, but I'll heal up." He'd had worse in his baseball days, compliments of a few wild pitches. And his knee had recovered pretty well, too, even though that injury had put an end to his baseball career.

She nodded, wringing her hands together.

He noted again how dead on her feet she looked. But not actually dead, which was good. Very good.

"Listen, I also wanted to thank you. If you hadn't come after me, I'm sure I wouldn't have made it back in." Her pretty brown eyes glistened with tears. "You saved my life. You're a true hero."

Her praise unnerved him; being called a hero... well, it wasn't necessary. He hadn't rescued her for accolades or attention. He'd rescued her because it was the right thing to do. "I only did what anyone else would have done."

"I'm not so sure about that," she replied, her tears welling at the corner of her eyes.

The tears in her eyes made his chest tight. Struggling to breathe, and make sense of his reactions to her, he again shoved away the urge to touch her, comfort her.

To be her emotional rock.

Whoa. That was not a place he needed to go. Emotional connections with women weren't his thing. Never had been. Not since Diana. Too much drama there. "I'm no hero, but I was glad to help."

She wiped at her eyes. "Well, I'm glad you helped, too. And my son certainly will be." She reached out and squeezed Seth's arm. "Because of you, he still has a mother."

His face went warm, along with the spot on his arm where she touched him. Thoughts zinged through his brain. She had a son? Was she married...? No, no, she'd been at the church *singles* event... Single mom, then. Okay.

He shook his head slightly, regretting it instantly

when the horses started stampeding again. He sucked in a large breath, trying to focus around the pain. "Again, I'm happy I could help," he stated.

Just then, Lily came out of the ladies' room to Seth's right. She, too, had slipped on a sweatshirt, but she looked as bedraggled as Kim. Her long blond hair was stringy, and her legs had sand all over them.

As she walked over, she nodded knowingly, looking at Kim. "See? What did I tell you?" She gestured to Seth. "He's okay."

Kim smiled, revealing sparkling white teeth and cute little crinkles around her eyes. Wow, she was pretty. Even when she was as pale as a ghost and fresh from a near-drowning.

Seth's knees went weak. From her smile and pretty face? Nah. He was just injured, right?

"That's a relief," Kim said. "The Lord was watching over all of us today, wasn't He?"

Seth didn't quite know what to say to that, seeing as how he and God weren't that close. He may have prayed for help earlier, but he knew crises made people do weird stuff—even pray to a God who had never answered any prayers in the past.

But he did know that he needed to get home. ASAP. His eyes felt as if they were going to pop right out of him. And the horses had turned into elephants.

Drew came hurrying back into the E.R. waiting

room. He put his hand on Seth's shoulder and spoke up. "You don't look so good, dude. We should go. My rig's waiting."

Just then, Drew's pager went off. He looked down at it, scowling. "Sorry. It's the fire department." Drew had been part of Moonlight Cove's local volunteer fire brigade for years. He pulled out his cell. "I'll call and see what they need. You gonna be okay for another minute?"

Seth nodded, then flinched. "No problem." He needed to man up and sit tight.

His legs shaky, Seth found the nearest chair, resisting the urge to drop his head into his hands and groan. Kim and Lily followed and sat down, one on either side of him.

Even though he felt like he'd been run over by a truck, he wanted to know more about Kim. Odd, but there you had it. "So, I take it you're new in town," he said. Wow. Nice line. Really suave. And why did he care about his suaveness, anyway?

"How did you know?" Kim asked.

Lily piped in. "Moonlight Cove isn't that big a place, and Seth was born and raised here, like me." She smiled. "We were neighbors growing up."

He wanted to nod, but caught himself in time. "I...*we* know just about everyone who lives here."

"Then you probably know my aunt, Rose Latham," Kim said.

Ah-hah. "Yes, I do. Lovely lady. Rose is one of the nicest women I've ever met."

"My son, Dylan, and I are living with her."

"Now that you mention it, I do remember hearing that Rose's niece had moved in with her."

Kim raised her eyebrows. "Where did you hear that?"

He kicked up his mouth into a bemused half smile. "Moonlight Cove has a thriving grapevine, which I can't get away from because of my business," he told her. "Occupational hazard."

"Your business?" Kim asked.

"I own The Sports Shack, on Main Street."

"Hmm. I've never thought about a sports store being gossip central," Kim said.

"The Sports Shack is the only sporting goods store in town, and everybody shops there." He snorted under his breath. "Old guys are worse than any quilting circle. They have to have something to talk about when they aren't trading fishing stories." Seth avoided all the idle chatter and socializing as much as he could, preferring to spend most of his time in his office handling the business end of things while his mom handled the customer contact.

Kim gave him a lopsided smile, dimples flashing, and pushed her hair back behind her ear. "News travels fast around here, then?"

He stared for a moment, again struck by her

fresh prettiness. Even though he was hurting, he couldn't help but smile back. "You have no idea."

Living here definitely had its downside for a guy like Seth—the downside being all kinds of small-town relationship drama. Drama that had also, unfortunately, been part and parcel of his childhood; his mom and dad had fought all the time. And still did.

And Diana? He'd been in love with her his senior year in college, and she'd told him she loved him, too. But the day after he'd gone engagement-ring shopping, she'd dumped Seth for his best friend. Now, there was a black hold of turmoil if he'd ever seen one. He never wanted to go to that painful place again.

Still, it had seemed like a no-brainer to come back to town and take over his dad's store when Seth had suffered a career-ending knee injury three years ago and Dad had been looking toward retirement.

Seth loved all sports and had a degree in marketing from Washington State, so it made sense to return and run The Sports Shack. Besides, his dad had built the business from scratch, and Seth and his brothers, Curt and Ian, had grown up working in the store. It hadn't seemed right to sell the place to a stranger when his dad had wanted out.

The clincher had been when his parents had

announced they were divorcing. Though the split had been a long time coming, his mom had needed support when she'd finally decided to go through with the divorce, and had really needed Seth around. She still did, so he stayed. She wasn't good at coping on her own.

Seth sat in silence for a few moments, and despite his best efforts to curb his compelling curiosity about Kim, he wondered what her story was. She was single, but had a son. What had happened to the boy's father?

It seemed tactless to ask; they barely knew each other. But he was intrigued by Kim. Very intrigued.

Maybe too intrigued.

Drew hurried back, his face grim. "There's a fire out on Old Mill Road, and I'm one of the only volunteers available. Unfortunately, I have to go."

"Don't worry about it," Seth said. "I'll just call my mom and she'll come get me."

"Didn't you tell me that your mom went to Seattle this weekend?" Drew asked.

Seth mentally slapped his head, and even that hurt. "Yeah, I forgot. Maybe Curt can come get me." Granted, his eldest brother was at work and he and Seth weren't close, but hopefully he could leave early. Ian, the baby of the family, lived in California.

"We can take you home," Kim said. She belatedly looked at Lily. "Can't we?"

"Of course."

Seth chewed on her offer, noting Kim's pale skin and generally exhausted look. No. No way. "I can't impose like that," he told her. "Besides, you've got to be beat after what happened."

She put up a hand to stop his protest. "You wouldn't be imposing, trust me. You saved my life. It's the least I can do."

Seth hated asking anything of Kim. Or Lily. Or anyone, really. He was usually the one taking care of people, at least in his family. But Drew needed to get going, and Seth didn't want to hold him up. So he looked at Drew, bit the bullet and said, "Looks like I've got a ride. Go take care of that fire."

Drew nodded. "What are you going to do about the twenty-four-hour deal?"

"What twenty-four-hour deal?" Kim asked, peering intently back and forth between Drew and Seth.

Drew replied before Seth could head off any talk about the nurse's "rules." "Concussion patients aren't supposed to be alone for twenty-four hours after their injury."

Seth glared at Drew for opening his big mouth. The last thing he wanted was Kim feeling responsible for him for the next twenty-four hours. Plus, he liked his space.

Kim drew her eyebrows together. "Well, then, we'll have to make sure you're not alone."

Seth opened his mouth to protest.

"Doctor's orders," Kim said, cutting him off before he could get a word out. She pointed at him. "Right?"

"You're right. I'll call my brother." Seth went for his cell phone in his pocket, but came up empty. He'd left his cell in his sweatshirt pocket on the beach. He rose, scoping out the nearest pay phone, but Kim stopped him with a gentle touch to his arm.

"I'm taking you home to my aunt's house, and I won't take no for an answer."

"You mean *I'm* taking you guys to your aunt's house," Lily interjected.

Kim inclined her head. "Right. Lily's taking us."

Drew interrupted the discussion. "I need to go, so I trust you guys will work this out." He put a hand on Seth's shoulder. "I'll check in when I can."

Seth nodded. "Thanks, Drew. I appreciate all of your help."

"No problem," Drew said, then quickly headed out the door.

Seth watched him go. The will to argue was

sapping out of him, fast. As much as he hated to admit it, he needed to get prone. Anywhere. He didn't have the energy to be picky. "You sure it won't be an imposition?" he asked Kim.

"I'm sure, and even if it was, I'd still insist. You saved my life, and I owe you. Big time."

Seth digested that. He wasn't sure he liked the sound of being so connected to Kim. But doctor's orders were doctor's orders and connected didn't mean *involved with,* right? Because that was the last thing he wanted.

"Will your aunt mind?"

She gave him a chiding look. "What do you think? She'll love having someone to take care of."

From what he knew of Rose, Kim was right. If anyone in Moonlight Cove ever needed anything, Rose Latham was there. Still...

"So are we all on the same page?" Kim asked, almost, it seemed, daring him to argue. Her unwavering, stunning gaze bored directly into him.

He wanted to keel headfirst into those gorgeous eyes. But suddenly another bout of wooziness overtook him and the floor tilted. Stupid concussion.

He sat. He looked like he wasn't going to get the space he liked, or any more time to mull over his decision. He let out a heavy breath, hesitating, trying to think. If he gave in and let Kim take care of him—for now—they'd be even, and it would be easier for them to go their separate ways. Sounded like a good trade-off, given the circumstances.

"Same page," he finally spoke, hoping he wasn't going to regret his rushed decision.

"Excellent," Kim said. "You're a smart man, Seth."

He wasn't really sure about her assessment of his smarts, but he was too worn out to apply more mental force to the question. Hopefully being helpless would be a temporary affliction.

Summoning every bit of strength he had, he stood again. Vertigo overtook him and he sagged. Kim was there instantly. She took one arm, her touch at once gentle yet solid. Awareness zinged through him. He tried not to think too much about how much he liked the combination. What would be the point?

Lily came up on his left side and took his other arm. He couldn't help but notice her touch didn't cause any zings. But, then, he'd known Lily forever; she was like his cousin or something.

Seth fought the urge to lean on Kim as they walked toward the sliding doors leading to the parking lot, reminding himself that he only needed her for the next twenty-four hours. And then everything between them would be dead even. Strictly casual. And definitely disconnected.

No matter how much the pretty newcomer intrigued him.

Chapter Three

Kim, Lily and Seth made their way up the crushed-shell path that led from the gravel driveway to the wooden stairs that ascended Aunt Rose's back porch. A stiff breeze blew Kim's hair into her face and the fresh scent of the sea filled her lungs. She could hear the roar of the waves breaking on the beach just one hundred yards or so from the ranch-style cottage.

Like a trooper Seth went up the stairs by himself, although Kim noticed he used the handrail, which she was pretty sure an in-shape guy like him wouldn't normally do. When they reached the porch, he turned, his blue eyes shining bright against the backdrop of his pale face. "You're sure Rose won't mind?"

"I'm sure," she said, sounding amazingly normal considering she almost melted every time he looked at her. Not good. At all.

And even if by some wild stretch of the imagination Aunt Rose did mind, Kim would convince her otherwise. She had caused Seth's injuries with her careless foray into the ocean. Taking care of him was the least she could do.

Before they reached the door, it opened. Kim's maiden aunt Rose stood there, her round face wreathed in a smile. Her gray hair was pulled back into its customary bun, her wire-rimmed glasses were shoved up on the top of her head. She had a spatula in her hand and what looked like flour on her cheek.

Rose's eyes darted from Kim to Lily to Seth, obviously taking in their injured, drowned-rat appearances. Her face fell. "Oh, goodness me," she said, her forehead creasing. Her concerned gaze held on Seth's bandaged head. "What happened?"

"Kim almost drowned and Seth saved her," Lily blurted.

Aunt Rose's eyes widened and her mouth gaped open.

Kim glared at Lily, then held up a hand. "Don't worry. Everyone is okay, but Seth needs to lie down and isn't supposed to be alone for a while, so I brought him here. Let's go in and I'll tell you the whole story once he's settled."

Aunt Rose, bless her heart, didn't argue. She was a deeply practical woman, and knew when to ask questions and when to just go with the flow. She stepped back, gesturing them inside. "Of course." As soon as Seth was in the house Rose hurried over and had him sit on the sofa.

Kim followed her aunt into the house, drawing her eyebrows together. "Where's Dylan?" she asked. He was usually first to answer the door when someone arrived.

"He's at Benny's," Aunt Rose replied. "The puppies needed exercise."

"Ah. Of course." Kim looked at Seth. "Aunt Rose's neighbor has a dog who gave birth to seven puppies a month or so ago."

"Nothing like puppies to keep a kid interested," he replied.

"Dylan could hardly wait to get over there after you left," Rose added.

"Not surprising." Dylan loved all animals, but dogs in particular. Kim had promised him that he could have a dog as soon as they had their own place. Another reason, among many, that Kim needed a job and her independence.

"I can't keep him away," Rose said. "Good thing Benny loves having Dylan around."

Kim was pretty sure Benny, a retired widower, had a bit of a crush on Rose, too. He blushed and stammered like a schoolboy every time he talked to her. Truth be told, Kim was envious of the awkward attention Benny paid to Rose. It made her yearn for someone of her own…but that would be a mistake.

Kim turned and noticed Lily holding back on the porch.

"Um…now that everyone is here safe and sound, I think I'm just gonna head home," Lily said, rubbing her eyes. "I'm pooped."

Kim knew that feeling. "All right." She went out onto the porch and hugged Lily. "Thank you so much for all your help today." She stepped back and gave Lily a gentle smile. "I appreciate it. I haven't really made friends since I got here and, well, I've been a bit lonely. Even though we only met today, it's nice to know I have a new friend." Kim was a social butterfly at heart, and had joined the church's singles group for friendly fellowship; it was high time her social life arose from the dead. Well, most parts of it, anyway. The safe parts.

"I'm glad I could help out," Lily replied, returning Kim's smile. "Call me if you need anything. I'm in the phone book. And remember, the singles group is having a progressive dinner in three weeks. You should definitely come."

"Sounds good," Kim said. Spending time with people her own age was definitely on her To Do list.

Lily waved goodbye and headed back to her car.

Kim noted it was raining now, the fine drizzle coating everything in gray mist. Funny how fast the weather could change in Moonlight Cove.

She shut the front door, noting that Seth and Aunt Rose had left the living room. Expecting to find them in the kitchen, she made her way through the cozy living room.

The smell of freshly baked cookies permeated the air—snickerdoodles was Kim's guess. With fatigue rolling over her in a wave, she headed through the arched doorway that led from the living room into the kitchen to the left, determined to see to Seth's care before she gave in to her exhaustion.

The homey blue, white and yellow kitchen was the heart of her aunt's house. Remnants of her aunt's cookie making session sat on the tiled counters…but Rose and Seth weren't there.

Frowning, Kim headed back out into the living room, turned left and went down the short hallway that led to the house's three small bedrooms.

Sure enough, Aunt Rose and Seth were in the first bedroom on the right, Dylan's room. Seth was already stretched out on Dylan's twin bed, and Aunt Rose was spreading a handmade patchwork quilt over him.

Rose turned when Kim walked in. "He wasn't looking good at all, so I decided it would be best if Seth, here, got some rest right away." She smiled serenely. "This seemed like the best place for him."

Kim was so glad her aunt had seen what needed doing and had simply done it. She silently thanked God for making her aunt so intuitive, nurturing and levelheaded. A blessing, really, and a much-needed balancing force in a life turned upside down by Scott's desertion.

"Thank you, Aunt Rose," she said. "As usual, you're right." She turned her attention to Seth, who definitely looked worse for wear. He must feel really rotten if he'd let her aunt put him to bed without any fuss.

Kim moved closer, resisting the urge to sit on the bed the way she did when she said good-night to Dylan. This wasn't her son, here. No, this was a full grown, very handsome, masculine man.

Warning bells clanged in her head.

She remained standing. "How are you doing?" she asked Seth.

He shrugged, then winced. "I've got a head-ache."

Her heart tugged at his obvious discomfort. "After the hit your head took, I'm not surprised. So rest is just what you need."

"I won't argue," he said, his eyelids drooping. Obviously the trauma of the day was catching up to him in a big way.

"Good." She smiled down at him. "Get some rest."

She turned away, but before she could leave, he reached out and grabbed her hand. His touch sent sparks shooting up her arm. Her breathing snagged.

"Thank you for letting me come here," he said, squeezing her hand, looking right at her with those gorgeous eyes of his, pinning her in place.

Kim's tummy flip-flopped. His eyes were *so* blue, like the sky in summer, clear and beautiful. Completely compelling.

Her heart fluttered and she forgot, very briefly, the past and the tough lessons it had taught her. Forgot that she needed to keep up her shields.

But then sanity returned and she forced herself to pull her hand from his warm grasp and look away from him. She needed to get a grip. Now. "It was the least I could do," she said. "You saved my life."

"I'm glad," he said, then closed his eyes, well on his way to a meeting with the sandman.

I'm glad, too.

Her legs shaking, Kim turned and followed Aunt Rose out of the room.

When they reached the living room, Aunt Rose turned around, gave Kim a quick once-over, then pulled her into a hug. "Are you all right, dear?"

Kim nodded, breathing in the comforting scent

of the lavender perfume Aunt Rose had worn for as long as Kim could remember. "I'm doing well, thanks to Seth."

Aunt Rose stepped back. "Why don't you go change into something dry and cozy, and I'll meet you in the kitchen so you can tell me what happened."

"Okay." Kim pulled at her damp, itchy clothes. "I feel like a piece of freeze-dried seaweed."

She headed to her room and changed into a pair of black fleece sweatpants and matching top, then padded down the hall to the kitchen, taking care to walk quietly so she wouldn't disturb the blue-eyed hero sleeping in her son's bed.

Rose smiled at her when she walked in. "You look like you need to eat. Why don't you sit down and I'll make you some tea and my special sandwiches. You can tell me what happened while I work. From the looks of things, it's quite a story."

"It *is* quite a story," Kim said. She could hardly believe the whole thing was real herself. "And sandwiches sound wonderful." Her aunt's mini peanut butter, honey and cinnamon sandwiches were a comfort food if there ever was one.

Limbs shaking, she sank down into a kitchen chair next to the table. Kim gazed at Rose while she worked, her chest constricting with affection and gratitude. With Kim's mom living in Hong

Kong with her third—no, fourth—husband, and Kim's dad out of the picture since he'd taken off with his secretary when Kim was twelve, moving in with one of them hadn't been possible.

And since Kim's only other relative, her cousin, Grant, lived in a tiny studio apartment in Seattle, going there hadn't been an option, either. The sad fact of the matter was, she'd had nowhere else to go when her ex had decided he didn't want the responsibility of a family any more and had walked out and obtained a quickie divorce six months ago.

Kim had used her small bit of savings to live on while she'd looked for a job in Los Angeles, but it had become clear after a few months that without a college degree, she wasn't going to make enough to pay both rent and child care any time soon.

Realistically, she needed a job, money and a degree. In teaching, if she had her wish.

So Aunt Rose had taken her and Dylan in, offering to take care of Dylan free of charge once Kim found a job in Moonlight Cove. College classes would follow when Kim could afford it.

Rose's help was great, but Kim needed to be able to depend on herself, and no one else. Otherwise, she'd be vulnerable again, and that…well that just wasn't an alternative.

"So, tell me what happened," Aunt Rose said as she set the teakettle to boil.

Listening intently as Kim told her the whole story, her face somber, Rose fired the tea and set the steaming cup on the table, along with a plate of sandwiches.

"Gracious," she said when Kim was done talking. "Sounds like Seth was quite the hero."

"He was. His bravery…astounds me." She swallowed and twisted her hands together, profoundly touched and deeply awed by what he'd done. "I never would have made it to shore without him. I'm sure of it."

"We can thank God for sending Seth out to get you," Rose said, sitting down next to Kim at the table. "This was His work, you know." Aunt Rose had always been a believer and was on the Moonlight Cove Community Church's council. It was no surprise she attributed Kim's survival to divine intervention.

"Oh, trust me, I've already given my thanks to Him." Her prayers had been answered several times today. Luckily, God was pretty dependable. Kim didn't know how she would have survived the unexpected disintegration of her marriage without her faith.

God would never let her down. Unlike men.

Aunt Rose regarded her for a long moment, then took a sip of tea. Very deliberately, it seemed, she set the mug down. "I need to say something," she said, her voice tinged with seriousness.

Kim froze, her tea halfway to her mouth. Ominous words. "Okay." She put her mug on the table, wondering what was on her aunt's mind.

Aunt Rose drew in a deep breath. "The thing is, I saw the way you looked at Seth."

Kim's cheeks heated. Ah.

She paused, thinking that she would have preferred to keep to herself how Seth's charm discombobulated her. Absolutely nothing was going to come of her notion that he was the best-looking, bravest guy she'd come across in ages. Mooning over him was pointless. And foolish.

"Do you like him?" Rose asked pointedly.

"Um…I don't know him well enough to like him," Kim said, scrambling to downplay the situation to Rose. Anything was better than admitting Seth got to her.

"But you do think he's handsome, right?" Rose picked up a sandwich and took a bite. "A woman would have to be dead not to."

No kidding. "I suppose," Kim said, hedging, although her aunt hadn't said anything Kim hadn't already thought. Seth was gorgeous. And unfortunately, Kim's judgment had always been disgustingly poor around handsome guys. Scott had been too good-looking for her own well-being. And look where *that* relationship had gotten her.

"You *suppose?*" her aunt said, her eyebrows high. She waved a hand in the air. "Oh, pshaw."

"You don't believe me?" Kim asked, trying to sound a bit offended to head off her aunt's suspicions.

"Honey, I was in the room with the two of you. I saw the look you exchanged, and the way you almost fell over."

Kim gazed down at the table. Guilty. There was no use denying she thought Seth was handsome. And she certainly wasn't going to lie. "Okay, so he's good-looking. That doesn't mean I want to date him. I'm not interested in any kind of romantic relationship. With anyone." Being left broken-hearted once was bad enough. Twice would be unbearable.

"Are you sure? Seth is very appealing…" Rose said, looking worried.

"Of course I'm sure. You know how devastated I was when Scott left." While their marriage had been rocky from the start—at nineteen neither one of them had been mature enough to get married—and they'd grown apart since Dylan had been born two years to the day after their wedding, Kim really hadn't seen Scott's abandonment coming. Or hadn't *wanted* to see it…

Another costly mistake, putting her head in the sand, hoping love would conquer all. Of course, it hadn't. Instead love had backhanded her.

Kim went on. "I can't put myself in a position to ever go through that again, and I certainly can't put Dylan through the loss of a father figure a second time." She frowned. "He cried every night for weeks after Scott left." Talk about gut-wrenching.

Rose's eyes softened, lit with sympathy. "I know Scott hurt you badly." She looked off into space as if she was in the grip of a bad memory. Something that had wounded her. "A broken heart is terribly painful. It's not something anyone wants to go through more than once."

Kim peered at her aunt, suddenly curious. "It sounds like you speak from experience."

Rose's eyes got misty. "I had my heart broken a very long time ago," she said, her voice coated in sorrow.

Kim's chest tightened, and she could hardly breathe. Obviously there was a lot of sadness behind Rose's revelation. "What happened?"

"Oh, back when I was young—a girl, really— there was a boy I loved. His name was Arthur." Rose smiled sadly. "Arthur Bennett. We met at a dance in town."

"Go on," Kim said. She needed to hear the story. Making a connection with her aunt via the pain of shared heartbreak seemed important somehow.

"His family was very wealthy, and mine wasn't. His parents didn't think I was good enough for him. They had a family friend's daughter in mind."

She drew in a deep, shaky breath. "He told me that he loved me, but then he married her instead."

A knot of empathy filled Kim's chest. She'd had no idea about any of Rose's past romantic turmoil. "Oh, I'm so, so sorry."

"Thank you, dear." She patted Kim's hand. "So, you see, I understand your wounds and I understand why you don't want to put your heart on the line. After Arthur left me, I never want to take that risk again, either."

So that explained why her aunt had never married. "Being alone is better than hurt and broken in two," Kim said, her chin raising. Rose's revelation had confirmed that belief quite well. Staying uninvolved romantically was the right path.

"So true, so true," Rose agreed, her eyes reflecting a lifetime of sadness. "And I don't want to see you get hurt again." She stood and started cleaning up the kitchen.

Kim sat back, gripping her mug of tea. Who would have guessed they had so much in common? Her aunt was more like her than she'd realized.

"Oh, I forgot," Rose said, picking up a large manila envelope from the counter. "This came in the mail for you today."

Kim took the envelope, scoping out the return address, her heart skipping a beat. "It's from the community college in Seattle."

"Are you still planning on taking early education

classes there?" Rose asked, gathering up the empty tea mugs.

"Yes, in time." Kim had put her dreams of becoming a teacher on hold when Dylan had been born, choosing instead to stay at home with him. She didn't regret that decision at all, but it was time to follow her dream.

"But not right away, correct?" Rose asked. "I'm not ready to lose you and Dylan just yet."

Kim smiled. "No, not right away." But eventually, she was moving to Seattle to be near Grant and to take advantage of the early education program at Seattle City College, which wasn't available anywhere near Moonlight Cove. For sure.

Rose picked up her glasses and put them on. "Oh, good. I've been lonely. It's wonderful to have you two around."

"It's nice to be here, Aunt Rose," Kim said, meaning it. She stood and started helping Rose clean the kitchen.

Rose shooed her away. "No, let me do this. You go ahead and relax. You need to rest."

With exhaustion pulling at her as if she had a rock around her neck, Kim agreed and headed to her room. She walked by Dylan's door, shivering when she thought of the courageous, handsome man who lay in there, asleep.

Unbidden, a vision of Seth's eyes gazing at her danced through her head, and her heart stuttered.

She'd wanted to lose herself in those eyes, let down her guard.

But she couldn't.

She needed to be smart. She needed to take her aunt's poignant story of her broken heart, blend it together with her own botched romantic history, and never forget the picture they painted.

If she did, pain was sure to follow.

Seth woke up a couple times during the night, kind of wishing he'd taken the doctor's offer of pain meds. His head hurt, period. But he was determined not to go down that road. He'd gut it out as best he could.

He'd dreamed that Kim was in his room at one point during the night, with the moonlight shining through the window on her face as she gazed down on him. He even dreamed that she touched his forehead, her soft fingers a gentle, soothing caress...

Finally he awoke and it was light out. His head had calmed down quite a bit. He had no idea what time Kim and her aunt got up, but he needed to be out of bed. Laying around just wasn't his thing. Besides, it was Monday, and he needed to get to the store and open up.

He'd gone to sleep in his board shorts and the T-shirt Drew had loaned him, so he threw the covers back, got up and blinked the spots away.

When he was steady, he folded the quilt he'd slept under and straightened the bed as best he could. Then he padded over to the wooden door and opened it.

A boy with sleep-messed blond hair, dressed in bright red pajamas, stood in the hall, looking up at Seth. The kid appeared to be around the age of six or so, but Seth didn't have much up-close experience with children, so he could be wrong.

"I've been waiting for you to wake up. My mom told me not to bother you, so I've been very quiet," the boy whispered.

Okay, this was Kim's son. "Well, you did a very good job." Seth held out his hand. "I'm Seth."

The boy put his small hand in Seth's and pumped it. "Oh, I know who you are." His eyes went wide. "You're the hero who rescued my mommy."

"Uh...well, yeah, I helped her out of the water." Seth had a feeling that, unfortunately, the dubious title of "hero" wasn't going to go anywhere anytime soon. Great.

"I'm Dylan," the boy said. "Dylan Hampton."

"Nice to meet you, Dylan," Seth replied.

Just then, Kim came down the hall. She was wrapped in a long, fuzzy pink robe over pajamas and had on fluffy white slippers. Her hair flowed in a dark river of waves over her shoulders, and her amber-colored eyes dominated her heart-shaped face.

His breathing snagged. He'd realized yesterday she was pretty, but here, like this, looking bright and relaxed, and not like a drowned cat, she was downright stunning. Pink was definitely her color, although he guessed she'd look good in ugly mud brown, too.

"Hey, now, Dyl," she said, her voice warm with a mother's love. "I told you not to bother Mr. Graham."

She moved closer and Seth could smell her scent, which reminded him of a clean ocean breeze, light and fresh. He finally managed to find his voice. "He didn't wake me up. He was as quiet as a little mouse."

Kim rubbed Dylan's narrow shoulders. "Good. He's been dying to meet you, so I wasn't sure he wouldn't just barge in and wake you up."

"How did you like my bed?" Dylan asked. "Comfortable, huh?"

In the haze of his pounding head and exhaustion last night, Seth hadn't realized he'd been put in Dylan's bed. It made sense now, but his mind hadn't been firing on all cylinders.

"Very comfy," he agreed. "Thank you for letting me borrow it." A thought occurred to him. "Where did you sleep?"

"With my mom."

"Don't worry," Kim said. "He loves sleeping in

my bed, which I suspect has something to do with the fact that he can watch TV in there."

Seth chuckled. "Not surprising at all. I always wanted a TV in my room, too."

"Auntie Rose made waffles—with chocolate chips," Dylan said, his voice full of excitement. "Because we have a guest."

Seth sniffed the air. He widened his grin. "I can smell them, buddy. Why don't you lead the way?" Actually, he was really hungry. Food would do him good right now. He needed fuel to get moving.

Dylan scampered off. Seth moved to follow, but Kim stopped him with a gentle touch to his arm that felt much warmer than he expected.

"How's the head?" she asked, gesturing to his bandage. "I checked on you a couple times in the night, and you seemed to be sleeping well."

Oh. So she'd actually been there, bathed in moonlight, touching his head. It hadn't been a dream.

He made himself focus on her thoughtfulness. "Thank you for that," he said softly. "But it wasn't necessary."

"Yes, it was. I had to make sure you were okay." She gazed at him quizzically. "*Are* you okay?"

"I feel more human this morning than I did last night."

"Great. Are you hungry?"

He stared into her eyes, losing himself for a moment in their topaz depths. "I'm sorry. What did you say?"

Kim blushed. "I asked if you were hungry. There are waffles in the kitchen," she gestured for him to follow her. "Aunt Rose loves to have people to cook for."

Fantastic. As a bachelor, no one had been cooking or caring for him lately.

He took her lead and walked down the hall, trying not to breathe in her appealing scent. He'd had enough of being light-headed. "Sounds good," he said. "Then I can get moving and get to work."

Kim stopped cold and Seth bumped into her, accidentally pressing his nose against her soft, fragrant, obviously freshly washed hair. He jumped back. Oops. Way too close for comfort.

She turned quickly around to face him. "What did you say?"

He paused. "That breakfast sounded good?"

"No the other part."

"About going to work?"

"Yeah, that," she replied, peering intently at him, two cute little creases forming between her delicate eyebrows.

He shrugged. "What about it?"

She crossed her arms. "No way are you going to work today."

Okay. So she was the bossy type. He didn't usually like that, but on her, bossy looked good. Go figure. "Why not?"

"You suffered a concussion and had stitches put in your head yesterday. You shouldn't be working." She pressed her features into a stern expression. "You need to rest. The doctor said so."

Him kicking back and resting were as likely as making it to the big league with a wife and two kids. "Well, I have a business to run, and I'm the only one who can run it."

"Isn't there anyone else you can call?"

"Nope. My mom, who usually helps at the store, is out of town. And my dad…can't help out right now." More like *wouldn't* help out, but there was no need to get into the dirty details. "It's me, or no one."

She chewed on her lip. After a few seconds of thinking, she said, "Why don't you let me go in for you?"

"No. Absolutely not. I can't ask you to do that."

"Why not? I need a job, and you need someone to help out." She smiled, her dimples peeking out. "It's the perfect solution."

He forced himself not to stare at her fascinating dimples. No, it wasn't the perfect solution. It was a terrible idea. She'd already done enough; they were even. Period.

Before he got words out, she added, "Besides, the doctor said you weren't supposed to be alone for twenty-four hours."

"It's a busy place," he replied levelly. "I'll be surrounded by people all day long. I'm guessing I won't be alone at all."

She shook her head. "You never know. Why don't you let me come with you? I could help out, and keep an eye on you at the same time."

"No," he said. "You've done enough." More than he'd wanted, actually. It was time to disengage.

She paused, gazing at him from underneath her long eyelashes. "Actually…you'd be doing me a favor, too."

He narrowed his eyes. Uh-oh. She needed a favor. "How so?" he asked cautiously.

"Well, I've been saving to take classes, and only need a bit more for one term of college, so I really need a job. You need someone to help out while your mom's gone. If you let me work for you, we'll both benefit, right?"

He let out a breath and looked at the floor, stalling. Oh, man. She needed a job. And he needed someone to help out if he was realistic about his limitations at the moment. The Sports Shack was a two-person operation, no doubt about it. He needed an employee.

Kim was right. Her offer made sense. And,

really, how could he say no without seeming like an ungrateful, heartless idiot?

He rubbed his jaw, wishing he had more time to think all this through. He didn't usually make important decisions on the fly. Unfortunately, the store had to open on schedule—if he remembered correctly, he had a delivery coming this morning. He didn't have a lot of time to be cautious.

"All right," he said, hoping he didn't regret his decision. "You can come help out…for now." He'd leave it at that.

"Great," she said, beaming. "Perfect."

He mumbled his agreement. Her working for him was mutually beneficial; he'd be providing Kim with something she desperately needed, and vice versa. The solution sounded ideal….

So why in the world was he so conflicted about working with her?

He looked at her, trailing his gaze over her face. She was smiling broadly at him, her gorgeous golden eyes sparkling, her clear, fresh-scrubbed skin glowing. She looked happy. And full of life. And so beautiful he could barely breathe.

The truth belatedly smashed into him. The reason he hadn't wanted to agree to Kim's deal was as difficult to ignore as a grand slam when the score was tied.

He wanted to casually date the appealing Kim, not be her boss. He gave a mental groan. Yeah. It was going to be a long couple of days.

Chapter Four

Kim spent her first morning at The Sports Shack rearranging displays and unpacking and shelving various sporting goods items that had just been delivered.

Seth, on the other hand, hadn't come out of his office once since they'd arrived and he gave her brief, general instructions on how to manage the basic running of the store. He'd even told her that he preferred not to be interrupted unless it was an emergency, mumbling under his breath that he wasn't feeling up to par. Of course, he waved off her concerns about his concussion.

No, he hadn't even ventured out to see how she was doing with the job, although maybe that merely expressed his confidence in her ability to handle things by herself. Fortunately, she *had* been able on her own to help the five or six customers who'd wandered in from the quaint, flower-lined boardwalk.

Despite Seth's standoffish ways, she'd made it a point to stick her head in his office a few times to make sure he hadn't fainted dead away from his concussion. He'd been a bit terse, though civil. But other than the contact initiated by her, he'd stayed sequestered, uninvolved with the sales end of the business. And her.

Guess he left the people part of the store to his mom most of the time…?

The bells over the door rang, and a tall, thin gentleman dressed in a multi-pocketed vest, some kind of pants with straps over the shoulders and a battered fishing hat walked in and went directly to aisle four.

Per Seth's instructions, she headed over to the customer. "May I help you?" Kim said to the older man.

The older man turned and gave her a rueful smile. "Probably not."

She pulled in her chin. "What do you need?"

He sighed. "I'm looking for the new Fish Master 1000 surface lures that were supposed to come in today."

"Fish Master 1000?" In reality, Kim didn't know one lure from another. Who would have guessed there were so many ways to catch fish?

But she had unloaded some kind of lures in the

shipment this morning. They'd been in a green and white box. "What color is the package?"

The man laughed. "Don't rightly know." He looked around. "Is Seth here?"

Kim cast a hesitant glance toward Seth's office, located down a small hall in the back of the store. He'd made it clear he didn't want to be bothered unless the place was on fire. "Well, he doesn't come out onto the floor much," she said. As in *never.* "Are you sure I can't help you? I rearranged some things, but I can show you where I put the lures we got in today."

"Yeah, I'm a regular around this operation, and I know that Seth tends to hole up in the back," the man said. "He's funny that way. Kinda keeps to himself around people he doesn't know."

Funny? And odd, in her book. Of course, she was a bit of an extrovert. And Seth? Well, he clearly wasn't.

Kim felt the need to explain about her lack of lure knowledge. "I'm not that familiar with the lures because I'm just filling in for a few days—"

"Oh, yeah. I heard."

She blinked.

"I'm Elwood Olsen, local, longtime resident," he announced.

Okay. "Nice to meet you, Elwood. I'm—"

"Kim Hampton. I know."

More blinking.

He chuckled. "The story's all over Moonlight Cove," Elwood said. "You're Rose's niece, newly arrived to our auspicious burg. Seth rescued you from a nasty ripper yesterday, and you're filling in here for his mom."

Wow. News traveled fast in a small town. Was there anybody who didn't know what had happened on the beach yesterday, or that Kim was now working for Seth until his mom returned to town? Coming from a big city like L.A., it felt strange for everyone to know her business. "That's right."

"Yeah, I know the story, so that's why I wasn't really expecting you to know too much about the new lures." He started walking toward the back of the store. "I'll just go ask Seth. Save you some time."

Kim followed Elwood, trotting to keep up with his long-legged pace. "Um…sir? I don't think Mr. Graham wants to be bothered." Unless a person was drowning. Then Seth would race to the rescue. Odd. But seemingly true.

"Oh, don't worry your pretty little head about bugging Seth," Elwood said, waving a relaxed hand in the air over his shoulder. "He's known me his whole life, so he won't mind me barging in and dragging him out of his cave."

Kim halted and let Elwood proceed. Maybe it

was good for Seth to have some interaction with a customer or two. It couldn't be healthy for anyone to spend so much time alone, in a tiny, windowless office.

Of course it was entirely possible Seth wouldn't take kindly to being interrupted. She only hoped he wouldn't blame his employee for letting Elwood intrude upon his solitary splendor. She needed this job, even if it was only temporary.

"Hey, Seth. Nice headdress."

Seth looked up from some busywork he'd been distracting himself with after he and Kim had arrived at The Sports Shack. The alternative was being distracted by his attractive new employee, and that seemed like a bad idea. He still wasn't sure he'd made a levelheaded decision about agreeing to Kim's "deal."

Elwood Olsen stood in the doorway of Seth's tiny back office, looking like he was on his way to the fishing hole. Of course, every day was a fishing hole day for the retired-and-loving-it former Moonlight Cove pharmacist. He was a true fishing nut if Seth had ever seen one, and around these parts, and in this business, Seth saw a lot of that breed.

Seth smiled. "Leave it to you to call this thing a *headdress*." He gestured to the bandage on his head. "More like a head *dressing*," he said.

"Yeah," Elwood replied. "I heard about what happened." He gestured with a tilt of his head toward the main store floor. Toward Kim.

Seth shrugged. "It was no big deal." The last thing he wanted was a ton of attention for yesterday's events. He wasn't a "look at me, I saved a woman from drowning" kind of guy. Pretty much the opposite, if the truth were known. The less attention he got, the better.

"I guess you know I kinda…got tangled up on the way to shore."

Elwood raised his bushy gray eyebrows. "Tangled up?" He scoffed. "Yeah, right."

"What, you don't believe me?" Seth put his hand over his heart. "Elwood, I'm wounded, I truly am. In more places than just one, obviously." Elwood loved good banter.

"Nice story, Mr. Former Athlete. I happen to know you didn't just trip over your own two feet." He shook his head, then readjusted his hat. "No sirree. You suffered your grievous injury rescuing that pretty gal, Kim, out there."

This conversation was to be expected. According to Lily, who'd stopped by earlier, the story of his "heroic act" was all over town. Not exactly what he'd wanted to hear, but that was the way of small towns. There was no use fighting the gossip grapevine in Moonlight Cove, as much as he'd like to at times. Gossip did more harm than good.

"You're quite the hero," Elwood added.

Seth grimaced slightly. There was that word again. He was no hero. Anyone in his shoes would have done the same thing. Time to nip the hero talk in the bud, before the whole town stopped by to pat his back. He moved the conversation into safer ground. "Looks like you're ready for some fishing. Is there something I can help you with, Elwood?" Wonder why Kim hadn't helped him?

"I'm sure you can. Since Kim's new and all, so I thought you'd know where to find the surface lures that you were supposed to get in today."

Seth frowned. "Aren't they on aisle four?"

Elwood shook his head. "Nope. Kim said she rearranged some things…"

Seth tightened his jaw. Presumptuous of her to move things without permission, wasn't it?

"I'll come scope it out," he said. Guess there was no way to avoid a foray out into the store. Meaning there was no way to avoid Kim and her pretty eyes and fresh scent and endearingly bossy ways.

Or talking to her about leaving the merchandise alone. The displays were arranged a very specific way. Always had been. He didn't like her changing things.

He rose and stretched the kinks out. His shoulders were tight, and his head still ached some, but overall, he felt okay. Things would be great—if he didn't have to worry about keeping his attention off of Kim. Or about the store being rearranged. Suddenly, his life—and his job—had become a lot more complicated than he liked.

Seth moved past Elwood and out into the main part of the store. He headed toward aisle four, Elwood following in his wake. When he reached the lure section, he stopped, perusing the display. Sure enough, the new lures were nowhere to be found. He frowned.

Just then, Kim walked up, a feather duster in her hand. She wore a green work apron with the words *The Sports Shack* embroidered on the front, and had on a long-sleeve white T-shirt and wore a pair of jeans that really flattered her trim figure, which Seth tried not to notice.

He fought the urge to stare. He was her boss. Not her boyfriend. He had to remember that.

"Hey, you guys," she said, smiling as if Seth had just brought home the pennant for her. Maybe a bit too brightly. "What's up?"

Seth swallowed. "Where are the new lures?" he asked. "Elwood is looking for them."

She pointed left. "I checked and realized I moved them to the end of the aisle and put up some extras by the cash register."

Seth glared at her. "That brand has always been in this spot."

She shoved the feather duster in the back pocket

of her jeans. "I moved them because they fit better with the stock that came in today, and I thought it would be nice to have some of the newer ones on more prominent display when customers check out." She raised her eyebrows and gave him a pointed look, as if to say, "That's just good marketing, isn't it?"

Excellent line of reasoning. As a marketing major, he should know. But it still didn't sit well that she'd changed the store without asking him.

He inclined his head. "I suppose so." He didn't want to get into a discussion about her moving things in front of a customer. He'd talk to her later.

Kim turned her attention to Elwood and cranked her megawatt smile to STUN. "Why don't I show you what we have. I think you'll love the new selection."

Elwood blushed noticeably, as if he was about to melt into a puddle of pudding right there in the middle of what, apparently, used to be the lure display.

Seth knew that melting feeling.

Elwood didn't stand a chance.

"O-okay," Elwood said, stammering like a schoolboy encountering his first crush on the playground. "That'd be good." He gave Seth an apologetic smile. "Sounds like she knows what she's doing, after all."

Words stuck in Seth's throat.

"Great!" she said, gesturing toward the front of the store. "If you'll follow me?"

The two of them walked away, Elwood trotting at her heels like an obedient puppy. Seth watched them head toward the cash register and the new display of lures now gracing the front counter.

He tightened his jaw, taken aback by the changes Kim had made. He'd rather things stay familiar.

Telling himself to calm down, he followed them to the front of the store, eager to see Kim...er, to observe his employee in her work environment. She obviously had sales communication skills. Yes. That was it. He was observing, just as any good boss would do.

On the way up, he checked a couple displays, noting that the bait display on aisle three had been rearranged, and actually looked better and more organized than it had before. There were new, visually appealing signs posted on the outdoor apparel aisle, the fishing vest display had been freshened and the worm bar had been cleaned. It all looked fine.

Still...if it ain't broke, don't fix it.

The checkout counter ran along the large windows that overlooked Main Street. At the moment, the sun was out, and he could see the lunch crowd gathering across the street at Palmer's Diner. Kim and Elwood stood at the counter, talking. Seth tried not to notice how the sun shining in the windows highlighted some copper-colored strands in her hair.

Instead, he homed in on their conversation while he casually straightened the perfectly ordered tennis ball display on the end of aisle one. He needed something to do that didn't involve watching Kim.

"Wow," Kim said. "Seth, did you know that Elwood has seven grandkids?"

So much for being sly. He looked up from inspecting a perfectly average can of hot pink tennis balls as if they held the secrets of the universe. "Oh, what?" he asked, trying to act like he wasn't eavesdropping. He put back the tennis balls.

And promptly knocked off five cans from the shelf onto the floor.

Busted.

Kim came out from behind the counter and hurried over. "Whoa, runaway tennis balls in aisle one."

Seth bent over to pick up one of the cans just as Kim reached down to get it. Their hands touched and his pulse jumped. He pulled away and stood, hoping he didn't look like his heart felt—as if it was going to hop out of his chest.

"I've got it," she said. "Why don't you grab the others."

He picked up the other cans and put them back. Then he followed Kim to the counter.

Elwood had a funny expression on his face, kind of as if he was keeping a big, juicy secret. He winked at Seth, grinning.

Seth blinked, but ignored Elwood's actions for lack of a better response. He cleared his throat. "Kim, you were saying?"

She returned behind the counter. "I was asking if you knew that Elwood had seven grandkids."

Call him silly, but he could swear she was blushing, too.

"Nope, I didn't know that," Seth responded. He knew what kind of lures Elwood used, but he knew absolutely nothing about the older man's personal life.

"Five grandsons and two granddaughters." She looked to Elwood. "That must keep you pretty busy."

"Yup, yup," Elwood said, nodding, his face beaming with pride. "They live in Atlanta with my daughter, so I don't see them much, but when I visit, it's pretty wild."

"I'll bet," Kim said, her face lighting up into a radiant smile. "I only have one child, but I think it would be great to have a big family. I adore kids." Longing entered her expression, and then she turned and looked right at Seth. "What about you, Seth?"

He froze and stared back. In all his years, he'd never really pictured himself with a woman long enough to have kids. He'd been too young with Diana, and it just wasn't a place he'd gone with any of the other women he'd dated. He liked to keep things casual. It was safer that way.

He rubbed his face. "Um…I'm really not sure. It's not something I think about much." Which was the truth.

"Huh," Kim replied. "I would think a guy like you would be eager to settle down and have a family."

He pulled in his chin. "Why?"

"Oh, you know," she said, fiddling with the lure display she'd moved up to the front. "I guess because you're young and…eligible?"

"I am?"

"Oh, yeah," Elwood piped in. "He's the most eligible guy in town. Everyone knows that."

Seth laughed, but it came out as more like a snort. "Nah, there are a lot of guys who are more datable than me." Why did he want to downplay his eligibility status to Kim? Maybe his head injury was keeping him from thinking straight. He'd been off his oats all morning.

Kim gave him a funny look, opened her mouth, then quickly clamped it shut. She then began studiously ringing up Elwood's sale.

"Not really," Elwood said matter-of-factly. "What with you being a former professional baseball player and all."

Kim snapped her gaze to him. "You played pro baseball?"

"He sure did," Elwood said before Seth could respond. He handed cash for the lures to Kim. "Three years with the Mariners."

Seth wished Elwood had kept quiet about his baseball career; sometimes his former athlete background got him more attention than he was comfortable with. But it looked like the cat was out of the bat bag, so to speak. And everyone in town knew about his history. It was only a matter of time before Kim got the story.

He spread his arms wide. "It's the truth. I bashed up my knee in my third season and wasn't able to play again."

"Oh, I'm sorry," Kim said, passing Elwood his change and receipt. "That must have been rough."

He shrugged. "Not really. The pro athlete lifestyle didn't really agree with me." He'd loved the game, but not the attention.

"Still, he's famous around these parts," Elwood said, grinning as he swung his gaze toward Seth "The ladies love him. He has no problem getting dates."

Seth cringed. "I wouldn't say that," he replied. Sure, he dated. But not *that* much. He didn't see himself as a lady killer or anything.

"Interesting," Kim said, drawing out the word. She nodded as she looked at Seth from beneath her feathery eyelashes. "I'll have to remember that you're a heartbreaker."

"Oh, no, I've never broken anyone's heart," Seth replied quickly. It had been the other way around with Diana. "Nothing like that." Though why he cared what Kim thought was a mystery.

"Oh, come on, Seth." Elwood tucked his lures into one of the many pockets on his fishing vest. "You're the biggest catch in Moonlight Cove."

Kim just stared at him, her eyes widened slightly. Disapprovingly? Maybe…

Seth bit his lip. He wanted to vehemently deny Elwood's statement, maybe have Kim's approval. Instead he laughed as if they were simply joking around. "Whatever."

"Don't let Seth's in-demand bachelor-ness scare you off," Elwood said to Kim as he headed out the door. "He just hasn't found the right gal." Right before the door closed he added, "As far as I'm concerned, you're just what he's looking for."

Dead silence reigned once Elwood was gone. An unfamiliar shot of dismay ricocheted through Seth. Elwood was wrong, and Seth wanted to set the record straight and deny everything the man had said. But he couldn't make the words come out of his mouth. Weird.

He looked at Kim. "That Elwood," he finally said, rubbing his foot on an imaginary stain on the floor. "Always joking around."

"Yeah, he's a regular comedian," she said, her voice tinged with what seemed like sarcasm.

Seth laughed anyway, trying to put a mild, happy spin on things, hoping to keep it light. And impersonal.

Kim didn't laugh back. Instead, she stared at him for a moment, then started straightening some papers on the counter. "No, seriously. Guess I've got the scoop now, huh?"

"It's not a *scoop*," Seth said. "It's just idle small town gossip." And being painted as the town Casanova wasn't the story Seth had wanted her to hear.

Why? He'd never cared this much about a woman's opinion of him. He cleared his throat. Frankly, giving a rip what Kim thought scared him as much as Elwood saying Seth and Kim were perfect for each other. That wasn't a place Seth wanted to go. Better to avoid the pain.

"That may be," she said. "But gossip usually starts with a small grain of truth, doesn't it?"

He had no idea what to say to that. He was

single. He dated, and hadn't wanted to settle down, and probably never would. Did that make him a lothario? Not in his book.

Luckily the bell over the door rang, and a woman and her three small kids walked in, saving Seth from a response.

"We'll talk later," Kim said with a pointed look, then headed over to help the woman and her brood.

Seth rubbed his jaw. Oh, man. Have a heart-to-heart, about personal stuff? That was usually about the time he bugged out.

Kim greeted the family warmly, and then sank down until she was on eye level with the three kids, who all had brightly colored stuffed animals in their hands.

She said something Seth couldn't hear to the one who looked the youngest, and the little girl held up a pink and white stuffed cow. Kim oohed and aahed. When the little girl handed over the stuffed animal, Kim started mooing in a silly voice while she held up the cow in the air.

All the kids giggled. Kim joined in, and her beautiful laugh ran over Seth like warm, soothing water. He stood, transfixed, as she took each animal from each child and imitated the animal in a funny way. The kids loved it.

Wow. She really had a way with the little ones.

The mom glanced at Seth and waved, jerking his attention away from Kim. He didn't recognize the woman—a tourist?—but he waved back anyway, all friendly-like, glad for the reminder that he'd been standing there, staring like a lovesick fool.

Not good. He swiped a hand over his face. The motion made his head start pounding again. Suddenly it seemed too warm in the room. Was he sweating underneath his bandage? Obviously he needed fresh air.

He walked to the door. "I'm going to get some lunch across the street," he said to Kim. "I'll be back in a few."

Her gaze darted around the store. "Okay."

At her hesitant look, he paused. "Do you need me?"

"No," she replied, lifting her chin. "I'll be all right without you."

He nodded, his jaw tight.

Taking her at her word, he left. She was a tough cookie. She could handle the customers—and anything else thrown her way—on her own. At least he hoped so.

He stepped out onto the busy boardwalk, breathing in the fresh ocean air, trying to cool down, and shake off the funk he'd been in all morning. He hoped he could find what he needed out here.

And get a handle on what he *wasn't* looking for.

And that, he reminded himself as he made his way to Palmer's Diner, was any kind of woman who needed him.

Chapter Five

Kim watched Seth hightail it out of the store for lunch as if he hadn't eaten in a week. The restaurant across the way was a busy place. He'd be all right. Even though he'd been acting her version of weird all morning, sequestering himself in his cave of an office, except when Elwood was there. Maybe working by himself was Seth's routine.

And, boy, hadn't the conversation with Elwood been awkward? Seth had looked kind of embarrassed by Elwood's revelations about Seth's former baseball career and had really appeared to be flustered when she'd questioned him about his extensive dating history.

Point was, Seth wasn't looking to settle down. Neither was she. Perfect.

Shoving her thoughts to the back of her mind, she kept on task and helped the mom with the three adorable kids pick out T-ball cleats for the oldest girl.

The mom and girls left with their purchase, and the place went quiet. Kim busied herself cleaning displays, doing her best not to think about Seth and his dating history. What good would that do her?

Forty-five minutes later, Seth came back in. He held up a white take-out bag. "After I ate, I got you a turkey sandwich," he said. "I made a guess and got it with cranberry sauce."

Kim was touched he'd thought of her. "Great. That sounds a lot better than the low fat yogurt I brought with me."

His company sounded pretty good, too.

Oops. She shouldn't be thinking that way.

He walked over to the counter where she sat. "Hope you like whole wheat," he said, digging into the bag and pulling out a paper-wrapped sandwich.

"Love it," Kim said, doing her best not to notice for the third time that day how nice he looked, even with a bandage on his head.

They'd stopped at his house on the way in this morning, and he'd quickly showered and changed into a pair of tan Dockers and a light blue button-up shirt that did great things for his pale blue eyes. He smelled good, too, all woodsy and fresh from some kind of light aftershave.

He handed her the sandwich. "I'll get you something to drink from the fridge in the back. What would you like?"

"A glass of ice water would be great. But I'll get it." She started to rise.

"No, stay put."

"But you're supposed to be taking it easy." And she wasn't used to being waited on. Scott had barely lifted a finger for her while they'd been married.

Seth held up his hands. "I'm not good at sitting around. Let me get your drink."

Kim sank back down, nodding, sensing that arguing was pointless. "Okay."

He headed to the back room, and Kim chewed on her lip. Being taken care of—even in this small way—made her feel special.

She shook the thought from her head. He was just being considerate, that was all. No way should she get used to someone putting her needs first; doing so would be one sure way of ending up hurt by expectations that never came true.

Better to depend on herself, and God, of course, when she was again on her feet and living in Seattle.

Seth returned with a large glass full of ice water. "Here you go. Why don't you take your lunch break now?" He pointed outside. "Maybe enjoy the sunshine."

"Would you like to join me?" she blurted before she could hold back the line from her brain to her mouth. Why did she always jump in without looking? Bad habit.

He paused for a moment, his eyes widening slightly. "Uh…I can't."

Kim blinked, surprised at the disappointment burning through her.

He gestured to the cash register. "Someone has to man the counter. Besides, I already ate. Remember?"

Her face flamed. "Of course. Silly me." She laughed awkwardly, sounding like a cross between a monkey and a goose. She clapped her hand over her mouth, mortified.

Seth grinned. "Now there's a laugh if I ever heard one."

"I have a problem." She gestured in the air with her hand. "With honky, ugly laughter, I mean."

"I can tell," he replied, his eyes sparkling. "And your laugh might be honky, but it's far from ugly. Actually, I kinda like the sound."

"You do?" Kim said, pleasure spreading through her. "I've been teased about my honking before." By Scott. And not in a good kind of way. His teasing had always held a mean edge that made her feel like a dork.

"I do," Seth said, looking right at her, his eyes hitting her full force.

Her tummy flipped, and she stared back. For a couple seconds, neither one spoke, neither one moved. The only sound she heard was the boom of her pounding heart.

Finally Seth broke the silence. "By the way, while I appreciate your efforts to rearrange the merchandise, I'd rather you not move the stock around without asking."

She stiffened. Guess he didn't like what she'd done. Why did that hurt? He was her boss, not her friend. It shouldn't matter. "Okay."

"The thing is, my customers are set in their ways, and it's better if they can find things right away when they come in. Plus, we only have room for so much stock. If things get messed up, um, *moved,* we might not have room for everything."

She nodded, swallowing. He thought she'd messed things up? "You don't have to explain," she said. "You're the boss. You can run the store however you like."

The bell above the door rang.

Seth stepped back, then glanced toward the door. "There's a customer. I'll take care of him," he said. "Take as long as you need to eat."

"Okay." She picked up her sandwich and water and headed to the rear of the store. "I, uh, think I'll just go back here."

But Seth was already focused on the customer.

Kim scurried to the break room, feeling foolish. And chastened for rearranging the displays.

Had she actually invited him to eat with her? And then honked like some weird animal? And then stared at him as if he were the most handsome, most considerate man she'd ever met?

Only to have him criticize her for some creative merchandising.

Obviously, he didn't have any trouble being the boss man—

Wait a minute. His attitude was just as it should be. She was letting her attraction to him get to her. It was his job to tell her what to do around the store. She needed to lighten up and not let him rattle her.

She plopped into a chair in the break room and dropped her head into her hands, saying a quick prayer for strength and good judgment.

Calmed, Kim unwrapped her sandwich, wondering what was wrong with her. Had she lost what little sense she had? At the very least she should have realized one of them had to stay at the counter and help customers.

She took a sip of water to clear her throat, which was obviously clogged with something, making normal laughter impossible. She'd sounded ridiculous.

But he thought her monkey/goose laugh was adorable.

No, no, no. Seth was her boss, she owed him, end of story.

Love equaled pain. And dependence. The opposite of what she wanted. Plus, she wasn't staying in Moonlight Cove.

Not to mention he'd kind of hurt her feelings with his criticism of her changing the displays.

But wait…why did his opinion matter so much, anyway?

Oh, no. She didn't like the sound of any of this. No doubt about it; she had to find a way to get a handle on how much she was drawn to Seth.

But with his fathomless blue eyes fresh in her mind, acting as if she wasn't attracted to him seemed like an impossible task.

Please help me, Lord. I need your guidance now more than ever.

"Hope that new rod works out for you," Seth said to Floyd Simpson, another regular and local, whom Seth had known for as long as he could remember. "She's a beauty."

"She sure is," Floyd said. "I'll let you know how the fish are biting at Boulder Creek."

"You do that."

Floyd looked around, clearing his throat. "Say, when is your mom coming home?"

Not soon enough, as far as Seth was concerned. "She's due back in town Wednesday, and to work on Thursday." Three long days to get through with Kim around.

Before Seth had watched her with those kids, and heard her adorable laugh, he'd thought maybe working with her without his attraction taking over was doable. Now he wasn't so sure. She was just so appealing. In every way.

Floyd frowned, looking crestfallen, then ran a hand through his thinning gray hair. "Oh. That's a long way off."

Seth peered at Floyd speculatively, noting his frown. A thought occurred to Seth. Floyd had been a widower for—what?—five years now, and had been coming into the store an awful lot lately. He'd spent a fortune on fishing gear in the last month or so—and Seth's mom always helped him.

Hmm. Did Floyd have a crush on Mom? "Do I sense you're…um, anxious to see her?" Seth asked, probing.

"Maybe," Floyd said, blushing beneath his fisherman's tan. "Just a bit."

Seth paused, flummoxed.

Floyd held up his hands. "Now I know it's only been two years since your folks' divorce, Seth, and how hard your mom took it. But it's high time she got herself back among the social hubbub."

All good observations, actually.

Floyd shifted his tall frame from foot to foot. "I thought I might ask her out to dinner and a movie this coming weekend. She's been talking about wanting to see the new chick flick that just came out."

Not sure if he liked having his mom involved in this junior high flashback, Seth chewed on Floyd's intentions.

Perhaps having a romantic relationship entirely different than what she'd experienced with Dad—namely an emotional land mine waiting to explode—would be good for his mom. In the end, Seth just wanted her to be happy. And Floyd was a good guy.

"Maybe she *could* use some company," Seth said, warming to the idea of his mom dating. "And movies are definitely the way to her heart." Yeah, going out a bit would be good for his mom.

Floyd beamed. "I believe I will ask her out, then," Floyd said. "She likes Fisherman's Landing for dinner, doesn't she?"

Good for you, Floyd. He'd obviously been paying a lot of attention lately. "That's her favorite place. She always orders the bronzed salmon."

"Thanks for the tip." Floyd saluted Seth. "I owe you one."

"Just make my mom happy and that'll be enough." After what she'd been through with Seth's dad, it was the least she deserved.

"Will do."

Floyd left, and all his talk about dating made Seth think about Kim.

He stood for a moment, then swiped his face with his forearm like he'd done when he was one of the boys of summer.

How in the world was he going to get through the next few days with her around? She was like a dazzling ray of sun shining through the clouds, warming him in every corner of his body.

He let out a heavy breath. There was no help for the situation. He'd said she could work here, and he wasn't about to deny her this job. So he'd just have to keep his distance until his mom came back.

Just then, Kim returned to the front counter. He took one look at her and it was as if she'd signaled him home.

Man, oh, man. Obviously, his plan to put her out of his mind wasn't going to be easy.

But what could he do except ride out the situation and hope for strength?

Kim spent the afternoon straightening the shelves and stock, and helping customers. She loved being busy and productive, and she truly enjoyed applying herself to a job she was grateful to have.

By three-thirty, she'd worked her way to the small gym equipment display, which included an inexpensive elliptical trainer and a monstrous treadmill.

She slanted a speculative glance toward Seth's cave. No question. He was avoiding her again. He'd gone into his office after lunch and hadn't come back out at all. She'd helped all of the customers, which was great—being an extrovert, she loved interpersonal interaction. But it bothered her that he was deliberately keeping his distance.

She was only interested in what he was doing because…well, it just couldn't be good for someone to hole up in a small room with no human contact at all. He had to be climbing the walls by now.

She eyed the treadmill, thinking the machine would be so much more accessible if it traded places with the elliptical. But the treadmill was huge. She'd definitely need some muscle to move the monster.

Fortunately, there was a very fit man around… who had a concussion. No lifting for him.

Gnawing a nail, Kim looked around for something nonstrenuous she might need help with. Her thoughts were interrupted by the door bells, announcing the arrival of another customer. This place was hopping today.

"Welcome to The Sports Shack," she said, heading toward where the customer stood by the display of water bottles next to the register. "May I help you?"

A short, stout, middle-aged woman with chin-length blond hair and wire-rimmed glasses smiled at her. "I need to buy a pair of walking shoes."

"Wonderful," Kim said, smiling in a friendly way.

"I always have Seth help me," the woman said.

"Okay. I'll go get him and have him meet you in the shoe section in the back left corner."

The woman nodded her agreement, and Kim spun on her heel and headed for the bat cave. Excellent. She now officially needed Seth's help, per the customer's request. Not exactly an emergency, but close enough. She hoped.

The door to the office was ajar. Kim took a deep breath to calm her racing heart. She couldn't let him get to her.

Knocking softly, she called, "Hello?" Earth to Batman.

"Come in," Seth said.

She pushed the door open.

Seth sat at his desk in the small, windowless office, a dog-eared catalog of fishing supplies in his hand. Paperwork was neatly filed in metal holders on a file cabinet next to his desk, but the top of his desk was spotless and didn't look as if he'd been working on anything. The only messy area was the wastebasket, which was filled to the brim with balls of paper, a few littering the floor around it.

Interesting. What, exactly, was he so engrossed in back here?

She leaned against the doorjamb. "I have a woman out here who wants to buy a pair of walking shoes."

"Okay. Sell her some."

"She asked for you."

He paused. "Um, I'm kind of busy."

"With what?" She gestured to the overflowing wastebasket, quirking a brow. "Your three-point shot?"

He actually blushed under his bandage, and, unfortunately, the extra color did nothing to detract from his attractiveness. "No," he said, inclining his head, his mouth tight. "I have a lot of paperwork to do." He gestured to absolutely nothing on his desk, then seemed to catch himself. He quickly leaned over and pulled a file from the metal holder and waved the whole thing in the air. "The...inventory figures need perusing. Can't you help her?"

Perusing? "Oh, no, I know nothing about athletic shoes." True enough. "I only know about designer shoes," she said, which was pretty much right on because she looked at the Nordstrom catalog and dreamed about being able to afford a pair of Stuart Weitzman espadrilles someday. "And, besides, she wants you."

He opened his mouth to reply.

"She's waiting in the shoe department." And then she did a quick about-face and went back out to the main part of the store.

She walked by the shoe department and waved to the woman, who was busy looking through their fairly extensive display of athletic shoes. "Seth will be right with you, ma'am."

The woman looked up from the sporty walking shoe she had in her hand. "Great. He's the best."

Tell me something I don't already know.

Kim stopped at the workout apparel aisle located right next to the shoe department. She pretended to be looking through the sock display while surreptitiously watching the shoe area through the shelves to see Seth in action.

She waited a minute or so, her head ducked at an awkward angle. Was he coming out or not?

"Whatcha doin'?" a deep male voice said from behind her.

She yelped, then jumped and spun around.

Seth stood there, leaning in, his hands behind his back. He was smiling in a way that she could only describe as sly.

Pressing a hand to her thundering heart she skittered away and said, "You shouldn't sneak up on people like that. You almost gave me a heart attack."

"I did not sneak," he replied, moving forward, crowding her space a tiny bit. "I walked right up. But you were too engrossed in…the *socks* to hear me." His tone and word emphasis suggested he clearly thought she hadn't really been interested in the socks.

And he was right. She swallowed, her face warming, and just barely caught herself from honking a laugh. He was way too perceptive. And too handsome and charming for her own good. Even with his bandage on.

No wonder the customer had requested him. He probably got that a lot.

Flustered, she picked up a random pair of men's tube socks from the bin and babbled, "Oh, yes, aren't these great? Very distracting." She smiled brightly, trying to sell her excuse and doing a mighty poor job.

"Right," he said, taking the socks from her. He gazed down upon the package, as if he were cradling a fragile piece of priceless art. "These have got to be the most fascinating pair of socks I've ever laid eyes on."

She nodded as her brain scrambled for a comeback. "In fact, I think I'll buy those for…my cousin. He's been looking for socks, and those… are his favorite brand."

Seth's mouth curled at one corner. "Well, I'm not one to keep a man from his favorite brand of athletic socks." With a lift of his brow, he presented them to her with a flourish. "My treat, of course."

She reached out for the socks, lifting her chin, hoping he didn't notice her blush. "Thanks. My cousin will be thrilled."

Then she remembered the woman waiting in the shoe department. She pulled her sock-filled hands away, trying to compose herself. "Um…the customer?" She pointed in the general direction of the shoes. "Over there?"

He blinked, kind of like he was coming out of a trance. "Oh, yeah." A pause. "I'll go help her." He turned and went down the aisle and over to the shoe department.

Kim dropped the socks into the bin and pressed a trembling hand to her still-warm cheeks. Was she playing with fire? Definitely. And she was going to get burned for sure. She always did.

Too late, she realized, she should have left Seth in his cave.

The next day, Seth stayed in his office the whole time, preparing spreadsheets for the upcoming biannual inventory. Kim seemed to be learning the stock and had only come back once to ask a question.

He was both relieved and disappointed that he hadn't had to deal with her, which left him feeling off balance and out of sync all day.

By the close of business, he was as gloomy as the gray clouds that had moved in overnight, bringing drizzle. Maybe he just needed rest, although, really, he felt pretty good physically given he'd bonked his head the day before yesterday.

Just as he was shutting down his computer, a knock sounded on the door. "Come in."

Kim pushed the door open. "I'm heading out, if that's okay."

He took in the navy blue raincoat she'd put on and the black umbrella in her hand, frowning. "Are you walking home?"

She nodded. "Yeah. Lily's car broke down, so she borrowed mine to go on a job interview."

His chivalrous side screamed foul. "I'm finishing up," he said, turning his monitor off. "Why don't you let me drive you home."

Smiling crookedly, she said, "Thanks, that'd be great. The wind has kicked up, and it's a bit chilly."

"That's how it is around here," he said, rising. "Sunny one moment, cloudy and rainy and cold the next."

"True. But I love the variation. Los Angeles weather gets kind of monotonous."

He gestured down the hall. "My truck's out back."

As she turned and headed toward the store's service entrance, he followed, once again noticing the fresh smell that wafted in her wake. An uncharacteristic curiosity overtook him. "How did you end up in L.A.?" he asked, glancing her way.

Her face clouded. "My husband had always wanted to live down there. We were young and clueless and thought it would be a great adventure, moving to the big city. On an impulse we took the plunge and moved down there from Portland right after we got married."

He swung the rear door open and stepped back to let her through, pointing toward his rig.

Conversation ceased as they hurried to the vehicle through the rain. He pressed the remote on the key fob to unlock the doors and they both quickly climbed in.

Once they were on their way to Rose's, he glanced at Kim, noticing how pretty her brown eyes looked in the muted late afternoon light. "Since you're here in Moonlight Cove, I'm guessing the whole L.A. thing didn't work out?" he asked, strangely wanting to know more about her.

"No, it didn't," she said softly, her tone rueful.

His gut twisted at the pain in her voice, even as

he told himself the conversation was getting too personal for his taste. But he'd asked…

She continued on. "When the construction market went bust, Scott couldn't keep a job. With no family around, we had some rough times, and Scott couldn't handle it."

Seth made a left onto Rose's street. "But you got through it, right?" he said, impressed by her resiliency. Obviously, she'd bounced back from a lot.

"Yeah, but just barely. If not for Aunt Rose after Scott left, Dylan and I would probably be living on the street."

"Oh, wow." Seth rubbed his jaw as he swung into Rose's gravel driveway. "Sorry."

"Don't be," she said as the truck lurched to a stop. "I learned a lot about being impulsive, and that I can only depend on myself. Guess that's the lesson God was teaching me all along."

He didn't know what to say to that, so he busied himself turning off the ignition. The only lesson he'd ever learned from God is that He didn't always answer prayers.

Before Seth could think of something to say that wouldn't knock her faith, Kim exclaimed, "Oh, goodness! Would you look at that?"

Seth glanced to where she was pointing. Dylan, dressed in a yellow rain slicker and black rubber boots, was tromping through the yard toward them, brandishing an umbrella like a sword instead of holding it over his head to keep himself dry. His hair was sopping and water ran down his face in rivulets, but he wore a huge grin.

Seth chuckled. "He's soaking."

"I can't keep him out of the rain. He seems to love it."

"Good thing around here, I guess."

Dylan reached the truck and came around to the driver's side. Seth hit the power window button. "Hey, little man. What's up?"

Dylan's smile grew wider. He held his umbrella in the air. "Hi, Mr. Graham! Cool truck."

"Thanks. It gets around pretty good."

Dylan craned his neck to see his mom on the passenger side. "Hi, Mom," he said, waving.

"Hi, honey." She leaned over to get a better look at Dylan, and Seth's heart rate sped up as she moved nearer.

"Aren't you cold?" she asked Dylan. The temperature had dropped when the rain came.

"Nope. Auntie Rose made me soup, so I'm all warm from the inside out."

"Ah, I see," Kim said. "Aunt Rose to the rescue, right?" She looked at Seth. "What did I tell you?"

Dylan's eyes snagged on the Mariners sticker on Seth's front window. "You a Mariners' fan, Mr. Graham?"

"Sure am," Seth said. "I used to play for them."

Dylan's blue eyes widened. "No way!"

"Way," Seth said, resting his wrist on the steering wheel. "Three seasons."

"Wow. C-o-o-o-l," Dylan replied, drawing the word out. "Can we play catch sometime?"

Seth drew in a breath, pausing. He usually liked to keep connections to a minimum. Would it be a good idea to form an attachment to Dylan, no matter how small?

But then he remembered his first baseball coach, Mr. Campbell, and how much of a positive influence Coach Campbell had had on Seth when he had needed it the most—just about the time Seth's family had become unstable because of his parents' fighting, making home more of a war zone than anything else.

Sounded like Dylan could use a Coach Campbell in his life, at least a little bit. Seth wouldn't be the one to deny him that experience. No way. Besides, he liked Dylan, and for some reason felt comfortable around him.

Yeah, the more he thought, the more he realized that it would be fun to play his favorite sport with a kid. Maybe dredge up some happy memories from his youthful baseball days, one of the few bright spots in his childhood.

Kim piped in just as Seth was going to agree.

"Dylan, Mr. Graham is very busy and I'm sure he doesn't have time to play catch with you."

Seth swung his gaze her way, narrowing his eyes. Why was she so intent on deciding stuff for him, anyway? "Actually, I do have time in the evenings."

She blinked, hardened her gaze significantly, then looked at Dylan. "And he isn't supposed to exert himself for a few days because of his concussion."

Oh, yeah. His stinking head injury. There *was* that…

He gazed at Dylan, whose grin had turned upside down. The kid looked downright forlorn with the rain running down his face.

Seth hated disappointing him; he knew too well how that felt, and he just wouldn't be the one to brush off Dylan like Seth's dad had always brushed him off. The sting of rejection still hurt deep down. "Don't worry, we'll play next week when I'm allowed."

"You mean it?" Dylan said, his mouth splitting into a gap-toothed smile.

"Definitely."

"Thanks, Mr. Graham. You're the best."

The best. A warm glow spread through Seth, unlike anything he'd ever really experienced. Surprisingly, it felt good to have a boy look up to him, admire him. Really good.

"Go on in, honey, and help Auntie Rose set the table after you dry off," Kim said to her son. "I'll be there in a moment."

Waving, Dylan scampered across the yard and up the stairs, splashing through puddles on his way.

Kim sat silently for a few seconds. "You didn't have to do that, you know."

Seth shrugged. "I know, but I wanted to." True enough.

She opened the passenger door. "Well, we'll see. You may change your mind later on, so I won't hold you to your promise." She started to get out, but Seth stopped her with a touch on her arm.

"I won't change my mind later. I said I'd play catch with him, and I meant it."

She looked at him, then down at her arm where he'd touched it. "People say things they don't mean all the time, and I don't want to see Dylan hurt when you don't have time for him," she said. "You can understand that, can't you?"

Oh, yeah, he understood. Too well. Seth's own father had never had time for him. Seth finally quit expecting much from his dad, but the damage had been done. He wouldn't do the same to Dylan. Not on his life. "I'll make time, trust me."

Her jaw clenched. Kim climbed out of the truck, then turned and drilled him again with her sharp gaze. "When it comes to my son, you have to earn my trust," she said in an even tone, edged in steel. "And that won't come easy."

Before Seth could reply, she slammed the truck door and dashed in the direction of the house, dodging raindrops.

Seth watched her go, admiring her protectiveness, even as he wondered what had caused her to distrust him. What had happened to make her so protective?

And the bigger question was, why did he care?

Chapter Six

Seth sorted through the tackle box display, looking for a new model for Jack Braden, the owner of Wind Riders, the kite shop three doors down.

Kim was on her lunch break, so Seth had taken over out front briefly.

"Who's the pretty gal working with you today?" Jack asked.

Seth glanced up. "What? You haven't heard what happened?"

Seth thought everyone in town knew the story about how he'd saved Kim's life three days ago and that she was now working for him. Nothing was a secret around here. He was surprised news of the events hadn't been on the front page of the Moonlight Cove Gazette in huge letters.

Jack, who was a few years older than Seth's age but hadn't grown up around these parts, shook his head. "Nope, I just got back in town from a buying trip to Seattle this morning." He raised a speculative brown eyebrow. "What's the story?"

Seth grabbed the new model of a single-latch, double-tray tackle box he was looking for and handed it to Jack. "Oh, nothing. I just…well, she got caught in a rip on Sunday, and I pulled her out." He tugged off the baseball cap he'd put on to cover up the bandage and pointed to his forehead. "I got tangled up with a rock on the way to shore."

"Wow." Jack winced. "That had to hurt."

Seth shrugged, then carefully replaced his hat. "Yeah."

"Sounds heroic."

"I just did what anybody would do," Seth said, holding up his hands. "The whole thing was no big deal."

"Okay, okay," Jack said with a laugh. "You don't want any accolades. I get that." He opened the tackle box and looked inside. "Still doesn't explain why she's working here."

The speculation in Jack's voice was clear to Seth. "My mom's out of town, so Kim's helping out. Nothing more than that."

"Ah, I see," Jack said. "So is she new to Moonlight Cove?"

"Yeah, she's living with her aunt, Rose Latham." Seth frowned. "Do I detect a note of interest?" Kim was very, very attractive, and Jack was newly divorced and now single. It made sense he might be interested in Kim. But the thought of Jack and Kim together sat completely wrong with Seth.

Jack shook his head. "No," he said, drawing out the word emphatically. "Not from me. Not after what happened with Karen." Jack's wife had left him for another man about six months ago, leaving Jack to raise their twelve-year-old daughter on his own. It was no secret in town that Jack had been hit hard by the betrayal, and his daughter, Cate, had been having a difficult time adjusting, too.

"Yeah, I hear you," Seth replied. "Relationships can really hurt, can't they?" As in cut you to the bone.

"That's an understatement." Jack closed the fancy tackle box, his eyes reflecting profound sadness. "I can't see myself ever falling in love again."

Though Seth hadn't been dumped by a wife the way Jack had, Seth understood his pain—and agreed with his reluctance to ever fall victim to love.

"Same here," Seth said. "Love...well, it's just not for me." That was his story, and he was sticking to the tale.

For some reason, Kim laughing her goofy laugh popped into his head. No. He shook it off faster than an underhand toss, then pointed to the tackle box. "Is that the one you want?"

Jack nodded and they headed to the register.

Just as they reached the front counter, Kim walked back into the store, a white take-out sandwich bag in her hand. She was chatting with a young woman with short, dark hair.

She continued toward the front counter, waved, set her lunch down and then led the woman to the fitness section.

Seth fought the urge to look at Kim as she helped the customer pick out a fitness ball. But trying to keep his attention off of Kim was useless; it was like there was a giant sunbeam shining on her wherever she went. Time and time again he found his attention drawn to her glow while he rang up Jack's purchase.

"You like her, don't you?" Jack said when Seth handed him his receipt.

"What? No." Seth cleared his throat and tried to look cool.

Jack grinned. "You were just staring at her."

Seth would have to watch that. "She's nice, that's all."

"Yeah, right," Jack replied, laughing. "And she's gorgeous. It's about time someone piqued your interest for more than two seconds."

"I am not interested in her," Seth said, fiddling with some papers. "You know I like my space." For good reason. And once his mom returned, he'd have that space once again and he could relax.

"I know, I know. But come on." Jack glanced at Kim.

She giggled at something her customer had said, her bright, happy laughter filling the air. Her gregarious personality was infectious, and Seth felt like he had a bad case of the happy germ she was spreading.

"How are you going to ignore her for long?" Jack asked.

Good question. "I just…will." Yeah. When baseball was played on a gridiron…

"Well, let me know how that works out for you," Jack said as he headed toward the door. "I think ignoring the obvious is harder than it sounds."

Seth stared at Jack as he left, getting jabbed by his words.

Uneasiness slithered through him. He needed to get out of here. Was it quitting time yet? He looked at his watch. Only three o'clock.

He turned to go back to his office, but the bells above the door stopped him. He'd help this customer, then go back to his hideout—*office*—for the rest of the day.

Unexpectedly, his mom came through the door.

"Mom!" he said, probably a bit too exuberantly. "I didn't expect to see you today."

"Baby!" Her forehead creased deeply as she hustled into the store toward him, her blue eyes on his bandaged head. "I heard what happened," she said, putting her arms around him and hugging him tight. The scent of her Jean Nate rolled over him in a wave. "Are you all right? I heard you had a hundred stitches in your head."

He scoffed. "I'm okay, Mom. And I got ten stitches, not a hundred." Looked like the Moonlight Cove grapevine was alive and well, and functioning with as much accuracy as a game of telephone.

She pulled away and looked him up and down. "What you did was very brave."

He waved her off. "Stop, Mom. Really. So why are you back early?"

She ran a hand through her short blond hair. "Edith got food poisoning from some bad oysters, so we headed home last night."

"Great, great," he said, smiling. Now maybe things could get back to normal around here.

"You think it's great Edith got food poisoning?"

"No, no. Just great that you're back."

Before she replied, her gaze locked on something. In the fitness aisle.

The corners of his mom's neatly lined lips tilted up ever so slightly. "Well, I'm not back, just so you know."

His stomach dropped. "What do you mean?"

She coughed suddenly and dramatically, sounding as if she was going to hack up a lung. In a badly acted movie about consumption. "I'm coming down with a cold, and won't be able to work…for at least a week."

He scowled, instantly suspicious. Seth wouldn't be surprised if his mom faked an illness to get what she wanted. Which was…what? Shifting his weight away from her, he eyed her critically. "What are you doing?"

She hacked again.

No way was that cough real.

"I'm coughing, can't you see?" she said, her gaze casting around the store. "I'm on my deathbed."

Seth looked her over. As usual, she appeared as fit as an All Star, thanks to her regular walking schedule and good genes. She had color in her cheeks and looked completely steady on her feet. In fact, she was the picture of health and could probably whip up a gourmet dinner for ten in an hour or so. And clean up the whole thing, too, with energy to spare.

He put a hand to her forehead, just in case his instincts were off. Her skin was as cool as cream. "Mom…"

Suddenly, his mom's sudden illness made perfect sense; she'd been home long enough to get the scoop on him and Kim from her friends. Yeah, there was that old gossip mill again, biting him, as efficiently as ever. Wasn't that just great?

Seth folded his arms across his chest. "I know what you're doing, and it won't work."

"What am I doing?" she asked, the picture of innocence. She was a good con artist, he'd give her that.

He looked right into her eyes, so like his own. "You're matchmaking." It was no secret that she wanted him married with kids. Yesterday. He'd never felt guilty about not providing her with grandkids; this store was his baby, and had always been enough for him. "I can tell."

She suddenly started digging in the carpetbag she called a purse, avoiding his pointed gaze. "Really, Seth, I have no idea what you're talking about."

Aha. "Yes, you do," he said, trying to catch her eye. He and his two brothers all knew Mom couldn't look at whomever she was trying to snow. "You're making excuses not to work so Kim has to work for you."

His mom pulled out a mangled tissue from the depths of her bag, then made a big show of blowing her nose. Complete with phony nose-blasting sounds that sounded like a dying elk.

Kim and her customer looked over, their eyes wide with obvious surprise, presumably to see why there was a croaking forest animal in the store.

Mom waved at them, smiling brightly, then

turned back to him. "Who's Kim?" she asked with a totally straight face. But her eyes were looking over his shoulder, at some point on the wall, not at him. Her "tell" was obvious.

Seth shook his head and let out a heavy breath. "She's the woman you just waved at," he said, trying for patience. "As if you didn't know."

"Oh, yes. Her." Mom leaned in, a conspiratorial expression on her face. "She's very pretty, by the way, and Edith says Rose does nothing but rave about her niece, and what a good mother Kim is." She smiled, her whole face lighting up. "You could do worse, you know."

Exasperation rolled through him. His mom was stubborn and very intent on getting what she wanted, even if that meant impersonating ill animals.

In reality, short of hog-tying her, there was nothing he could do about getting her back to work. Wonderful.

"I know better than to try to change your mind," he said. Arguing would be pointless, and he didn't have the energy for an quarrel at the moment. Conflict just wasn't his thing.

"Of course you do." Mom patted his arm.

She knew him too well.

"Toodle-loo," she said. "I've got to head out. I'll call you when I'm well."

She hustled out in a cloud of Nate with a spring

in her step that had everything to do with, Seth was sure, the fact that her plot to shove him and Kim together had been hatched.

Seth stood there, shell-shocked. Suddenly Jack's parting words seemed prophetic.

Ignoring the obvious was harder than it sounded.

Yeah. No matter how he cut the sentiment, Jack's shrewd statement just didn't bode well for Seth.

"Hey, Mom!"

At the sound of Dylan's voice, Kim looked up from the computer on the front counter and the CLEARANCE ITEM sign she was designing on her fourth day of work. Who would have guessed she'd get to use her creative side at this job? Very cool.

Dylan, wearing jeans, a navy blue T-shirt and what looked to be a quart of strawberry ice cream on his face, ran toward her. Aunt Rose followed close behind, decked out in her trademark daisy-adorned straw sun hat.

"Hey, Dyl," Kim said, smiling. "How's my little man?"

He flung himself in her arms and she held him tight, savoring the smell of sunshine, fresh ocean air and strawberry clinging to him. Simply wonderful.

"I'm great," he said. "Auntie Rose and I just got ice cream at I Scream for Ice Cream."

Kim leaned back, grinning, her heart happy. My, oh, my, she loved this little boy. "I can tell," she said, tweaking his nose. "You're wearing most of it."

"I tried to clean him up, but he was so anxious to get here and pick out his baseball equipment, he wouldn't hold still for a second," Rose said. "He practically ran the last block here."

"No worries," Kim replied. "Ice cream isn't permanent."

Aunt Rose said, "Do you mind if I run to the grocery store while you guys get his baseball items together?"

"No problem," Kim said. "Take as long as you need."

Rose turned and walked out the door.

"Where's Mr. Graham?" Dylan asked, his voice full of excitement. He craned his neck to look around the store, then jumped in the air a couple times to try to see over the display shelves. "He's going to help me pick out my stuff, isn't he?"

Kim bit her lip. She hadn't had the heart last night to tell Dylan that Seth didn't usually work out front. Her mistake. Ever since Dylan had found out that day in the rain that Seth used to play pro baseball, he'd been obsessed with having a "real" ballplayer help him pick out his gear. Looked like he wasn't going to let this go without a fight.

Kim put her hands on her hips. "Um, he's... working in back. He's busy." And after what had happened in what Kim now thought of as The Sock Incident, she had decided it was safer if Seth stayed in his office, working on his wastepaper basketball game.

She'd even gone so far as to vow to herself— out loud, before going to bed last night—that she had to do the prudent thing and quit being so fascinated by Seth. For her own self-preservation. Period.

"I'll go get him," Dylan exclaimed. "He can't be too busy for me."

Before Kim could catch Dylan, he'd turned and sprinted toward the back of the store. He was quick for a little guy, and left her in the dust.

"Dylan, come back here," she said, taking off after him. "Don't bother Mr. Graham."

Just as she rounded the corner of aisle four, Seth and Dylan collided at the entrance to the back hallway.

"Whoa, bud!" Seth said, lifting up Dylan under the arms as if he weighed nothing. "Where're you going?"

"Mr. Graham!" Dylan shouted. "I'm here!"

Kim stepped forward, holding out a hand in

apology. "I'm so sorry he's bothering you." She smiled sheepishly. "He got away from me."

Seth smiled back in what appeared to be a genuine way, and put Dylan down. "He's no bother. We're chocolate chip waffle buddies, right?" Seth looked Dylan over, then pointed to his ice-cream-dotted shirt. "Looks like you've been eating goodies without me, though."

"Yup. That's ice cream. Auntie Rose took me to get some." He puffed out his chest. "I had two scoops."

"Two whole scoops? All by yourself?" Seth gave a mock-sad expression. "And you didn't invite me?"

"You can go next time," Dylan said, patting his arm. "Okay?"

Seth's face softened even more. "Sounds good."

Not to Kim. Playing "family" didn't sound agreeable at all. As attractive as Seth was, she refused to grow attached to him, and she didn't want Dylan to, either.

"Did you guys need something?" Seth looked right at Kim and raised his eyebrows. "Maybe like…socks?" he asked, his mouth quirking.

Kim's face heated, and words stuck in her throat. The Sock Incident just wasn't going to go away, was it?

Dylan piped in before Kim could get her

thoughts together. "Yeah, I need baseball socks," he said, completely oblivious. "And all the other baseball stuff."

Seth shifted his gaze to Dylan. "You on a team?"

Dylan nodded proudly. "Yup. Mom just signed me up for summer league. Practices start next week."

"Hey, that's great," Seth said, scruffing Dylan's blond head. "I started playing baseball when I was just about your age."

"And you played for the Mariners when you grew up, so that makes you an expert, right?"

Seth put his hands on his hips and cocked his head. "Yeah, I guess it does." He leaned down toward Dylan and whispered loudly, "I'm your guy."

"Great!" Dylan said, jumping up and down. "I bet I'm the only kid on my team to have a real baseball player help him."

Kim stepped forward and put a hand on Dylan's narrow shoulder. She was reluctant to burst his bubble by reminding him that The Sports Shack was the only sporting goods store in town, so all the kids got their gear here. Instead she focused on not letting Dylan get too attached to a guy who seemed to prefer holing up in his office most of the time rather than interacting with humans.

"Dylan," she said, trying to sound firm and

loving at the same time. "Mr. Graham is busy. I can help you pick out your stuff." She looked at Seth, trying to be nonchalant. "Don't worry about us. I can figure it out."

Dylan's shoulders slumped. "But Mom. I want a pro to help me."

A *male* pro?

Kim's heart just about broke in two. Dylan, she knew, was really missing a male influence in his life, and she would like nothing better than to help her son with such a vital absent piece. But hanging around Seth? Not the way to go. "Please, Dyl, don't argue," she said, trying to keep the quaver from her voice.

Seth paused, staring at Kim. He then mouthed, "It's okay."

Maybe for you, but not for me. Or Dylan.

Before Kim could come up with a response, Seth squatted down so he was at Dylan's eye level. "How about this? Why don't we both help you," he said, gesturing between himself and Kim. "Then you'll have two expert opinions."

"But my mom isn't an expert on baseball," Dylan said, frowning. "You are."

Seth rose. "No, but she's an expert on you, right?"

Warmth spread through Kim's chest.

"Yeah, I guess she is," Dylan said, nodding slowly. "She knows what size my feet are."

Seth had a point, but Kim still wasn't sold on Dylan getting attached to Seth. Trouble, if you asked her.

"Then it's settled." Seth gestured to the team sports section. "Why don't you go over and start looking. I'll be there in a moment."

"Cool!" Dylan squealed. "I've always wanted a baseball uniform and glove." His face wreathed in a bright smile, he scampered in the direction Seth had pointed.

Kim watched him go, biting her lip. She could see the hero worship in Dylan's eyes; the last thing she wanted to do was set him up to be hurt by another father figure. She needed to protect Dylan. Always.

Trouble was, how did she explain that to Seth without looking like she already had her and him halfway to the altar? Which she certainly didn't.

She looked at Seth. "You don't have to do this," she said, the words weaker than she intended. "Really."

"I know," he replied softly. "But I want to. I remember how excited I was to pick out my baseball gear when I was about his age." He shrugged. "Besides, he's hard to say no to."

No kidding.

Chewing on the inside of her lip, working up the guts to say no, she slanted a glance to Dylan.

"Come on, you guys," he said, literally glowing

with joyous anticipation. He motioned them in his direction. "I found a glove I like!"

Instantly, all of her common sense caved in the face of her son's happiness. How could she deny him? "Yes, he is hard to resist," she replied, resigned, but still wary. "Impossible, actually."

And so, unfortunately, was Seth.

After today, she promised, she'd have to find a way to defend against both of them.

But how?

Chapter Seven

"There you go, bud," Seth said to Dylan. He pressed on the toes of Dylan's brand-new baseball cleats. "Those look like they fit perfectly."

Kim stood back, watching big, athletic Seth squatting down low, fitting her son's kid-size baseball shoes with infinite gentleness and care.

Her breath caught, and for about the fourth time in the last half hour, her heart almost melted.

Dylan danced around, completely outfitted from head to toe in his brand-spanking-new blue and white baseball uniform. "This is so cool!" he said. "Thanks, Mr. Graham." Dylan looked adorable. She couldn't wait to see him on the field.

Seth rose and gave him a high five. "My pleasure, Dylan. You look great."

"Can we still play catch sometime?" Dylan asked eagerly, holding his gloved hand high in the air. "I need to practice a lot before the first game."

"Now, Dylan, sweetie," Kim said, needing to nip this lovefest in the bud. "Mr. Graham doesn't have time to play with you, and he's not your coach."

Dylan's face fell. He looked at Seth, his big blue eyes huge in his face.

Kim felt about an inch tall.

"Don't worry. I told you before, I'll find time, just as soon as the doc clears me," Seth said, touching Dylan's thin arm with his big hand. He then quickly backed up with the grace of an athlete and pretended to throw a baseball. "Maybe I can show you a few moves."

"That'd be awesome!" Dylan replied, belatedly catching the imaginary baseball.

Not so much, Kim thought, her heart both sinking and lifting at the same time. Confusing. Never mind how much she liked to watch Seth move.

Whoa. This was too much all at once. She needed to get back to work, away from Dylan and Seth's bonding moments. She'd deal with Dylan later. Surely she could put him off of wanting to spend more time with Seth. Then again, maybe not…

She stepped forward, inserting herself between Seth and her son, and made a *T* with her hands. "Okay, guys. Time-out."

They both looked at her. Killjoy.

Well, a mom had to do what a mom had to do. And a woman guarding her heart and her son... same story.

She bent down and retrieved the stack of baseball clothes and gear they'd picked out just as the bells over the door rang. "Mr. Graham and I need to get back to work, honey," she said to Dylan. "There's a customer here."

Before she could actually witness her son's anticipated crestfallen expression, she turned to Seth and gave him a pointed look. "Here." She dumped the pile of stuff in his arms. "Would you mind taking this up to the front of the store? I'll be right there."

Seth took the merchandise from her, opening his mouth for a moment, looking as if he wanted to argue. But then he seemed to understand her nonverbal language. He quickly clamped his lips shut, nodding once, and headed toward the register. Good.

A few moments passed while Kim gathered her conflicting thoughts.

"Mom," Dylan said, his voice filled with disappointment. "Why don't you want Mr. Graham to teach me how to play baseball?"

Because I don't want you to get hurt.

Kim closed her eyes for a moment, praying for the strength and wisdom to explain this to Dylan without divulging the exact reason for interrupting him and Seth—which he wouldn't understand, anyway—and without sounding completely heartless.

Tricky, for sure. But wasn't bobbing and weaving what parenting was all about? And she had to do it all alone.

So be it. She wanted her independence, would have it soon enough when she moved to Seattle. She could deal on her own.

Before she could respond with a believable answer, Aunt Rose walked up.

Ah. So her aunt was the customer. Good timing.

"Dylan," Rose said. "We need to let your mom and Mr. Graham get back to work."

Dylan stuck out his chin. "But—"

"And, remember? Benny is waiting for you to come exercise the puppies with the new toy we bought at Bow Wow Boutique," Rose replied matter-of-factly. "We better not keep him waiting."

"Oh, yeah," Dylan said, his eyes lighting up. He adored those puppies. "I forgot about that." He went over and took Rose's hand. "Let's go."

Kim gave Rose a look of gratitude. "Okay. And remember, I'm taking inventory here tonight, so I won't be home until late."

She hugged Dylan, then hastily said goodbye. As she watched them head out the door and into the summer sunshine, she breathed a sigh of relief.

Thank goodness she was safe from Dylan's questions, and from watching him idolize Seth.

But how long would that bubble of safety last?

Not long. Dylan was already clearly attached to Seth and obviously looked up to him. Her son needed a man in his life. Kim knew that, and needed to somehow provide that for Dylan, maybe through church and being on a baseball team. But not by spending time with Seth. He was too dangerous. Too likely to walk away and leave them both in the dust.

How in the world was she going to explain to Dylan why he and his new hero couldn't spend any time together?

Good question. Too bad she didn't have an answer she liked.

"I thought we might eat before we get started," Seth said, holding up a fragrant bag of food from Ellie's Café, a block down on Main. "I have two burgers and enough French fries to give an elephant a coronary."

Kim looked up at him from the laptop computer she'd been working on all day, her topaz-shaded eyes widening. She blinked. "You brought dinner?"

He shrugged. "It's dinnertime, and we've got to eat, right?" Right. "We need fuel so we can work on the inventory."

Good rationalization. He frowned. There was that pesky voice way in the back of his head again, the one that had been bugging him since he'd helped Dylan pick out his baseball stuff.

He mentally shushed the voice. He could handle being around Kim. No problem. Except for helping Dylan—it was his job, after all—he'd managed to stick to his plan and stay in his office the rest of the day.

"I guess you're right," she said, standing and stretching. "And I'm starved."

He forced his eyes to stay on her face, which wasn't hard; she looked very pretty today, all dark hair, flawless skin and sparkling eyes. Very pretty indeed.

"Good," he said, surprised he could talk at all given the way his attention was focused on the delightful details of Kim's face. He gave his head a small shake. "I…uh, put the Closed sign up. We can eat in the back."

"You know," she said, her gaze roaming to the windows. "It's a beautiful evening, and I could use some spa…er, air. Why don't we go to the park?"

"Good idea." Great, actually. The park was only a block away, and it was next to the beach. Wide, open space was always good. "I could stand to get out and blow the stink off, too."

She gave him a funny look. "What did you say?"

"You know? Get outside, blow the stink off?"

"I've never heard that expression," she said, throwing him a sideways look.

"My family has a saying about when someone needs to get outside." He made a motion in the air with his hands. "As in, they've been cooped up too long?"

She thought about that for a second, a cute little crease forming between her eyebrows. "Oh, I see. Good." A teasing light entered her eyes. "For a minute there I thought maybe you were implying that I stink."

"Oh, no, no, no. You smell wonderful," he said, the words coming out before he had a chance to rework his thoughts.

She froze, her face coloring in a very appealing way. "I do?"

"I mean, I'm sure, if I...um, were to smell you, you know, you wouldn't stink at all..." He trailed off. What in the world was wrong with him, anyway?

Silence dominated for a long, significant moment, as his clumsy attempt to justify his comment hung in the air.

Finally, Kim cleared her throat, breaking the awkward silence. "Thanks so much," she said, her voice tinged with mirth. "I can rest easy now, knowing I smell wonderful."

He peered at her, and saw that the teasing light

had come back into her eyes. She was cutting him a break, reducing what he'd said to a mere joke. Letting him off easy.

Something passed between them, and he felt her pull from five feet away, across the counter. She seemed to sway toward him, and he actually took a half step in her direction before he could think.

But sanity swooped in at the last second, smothering his attraction like a baseball glove on a fast grounder. He grabbed on to his control like a vise. He was hungry and tired, and he'd been cooped up in back all day. That was all. "Why don't we go have our picnic?"

She gave a single, definitive nod. "I'll get my purse and grab a couple waters from the fridge." And then she disappeared down the aisle and went into the back room.

Uneasy, Seth took the opportunity to regroup. He removed his hat, caught himself before he could scratch his injury, then carefully put his hat back on over his bandage.

Man, she kept him off balance.

A few minutes later, they were walking down the boardwalk to the park. The sun was beginning its descent and hung over them to the left like a big yellow ball of honey. The warmth of the beautiful day remained, but the coastal breeze, as always, persisted, cooling things off a bit.

Seth stayed quiet as they walked. He cast periodic, surreptitious looks her way, enjoying the way the wind blew her hair around her face like a dark cloud and how the waning sun turned her creamy skin to molten gold.

They reached the park, which consisted of a grassy area, a state-of-the-art play structure and several picnic tables lining the edge near the beach.

"Look at those kids." Kim pointed in the direction of the play area. "Aren't they cute?"

She's the cute one.

Without saying that, Seth turned his attention to where she'd pointed. Several rambunctious kids around Dylan's age were hanging, tummies down, on the swings. Two women sat nearby on a bench, supervising. Obviously, the moms.

The kids' happy, carefree giggles filled the air, and somehow the sound made him feel happy and carefree, too, for the first time in recent memory. Funny, he'd never paid attention to any children in this park before.

"Yeah, they are cute," he said, actually meaning it. "Does Dylan come here to play?"

She nodded. "He loves this park."

"We'll have to bring him here to goof around sometime," he exclaimed without thinking. Oh, man. Had he really said that?

Kim was silent for a long moment. "Really?"

The imagined picture of Dylan and Kim here with him looked better than he'd thought it would. "Sure." Seth was a big boy; a playdate with a seven-year-old wasn't *that* threatening.

She didn't respond right away, and her expression turned inscrutable.

"Would that be okay with you?" he asked. Maybe she wouldn't want to come here with him…?

"We'll see." She tucked her hair behind her ear. "Dylan would love it, I'm sure, but…" She trailed off, shrugging.

There was her mistrust of him again.

Guess he'd just have to prove her wrong.

They sat down across from each other at the picnic table and got out the food. Seth dug into his burger and the big bag of fries he'd ordered for them to share. For a while they sat there in companionable silence, eating, and he forced himself not to stare at Kim.

A gull flew overhead, its call whipping away on the wind. Another gull flew close, dipping and soaring, and then they flew off together, out over the ocean, their wings flapping in perfect sync.

Kim watched the birds, her face glowing, her mouth pulled up into a stunning smile that took away his breath all over again. She then turned slightly from him and gazed out toward the ocean for a long minute, holding her windblown hair in her hand, her face serene.

"So." She turned back toward him, then rested her chin in her hand. "How was it growing up in a beautiful place like Moonlight Cove?"

He tensed up. "It was…okay," he replied with a casual shrug, which was mostly true. The Moonlight Cove part had been okay. His dysfunctional family part…not so much.

"Do I sense some hesitation?" she asked, pinning him in place with her inquisitive eyes. "A story, maybe?"

He picked up a fry and concentrated on loading it with just the right amount of ketchup, avoiding her scrutiny. He surprised himself by saying, "Maybe."

"You want to tell me about it?" she asked, her voice soft and compelling. "I'm a good listener."

She gazed at him with what looked like understanding, her expression alight with unselfish caring. "I know we don't know each other very well," she continued on when he didn't respond. "But sometimes it helps to talk about things, you know?"

He swiped a hand over his face, struggling with her candidness. He didn't really like to talk about his childhood. Doing so always brought up painful memories, along with some good old-fashioned shame. His family wasn't like other families. Embarrassing.

"I'm not a big talker," he said. "I don't like to get all touchy-feely."

"I figured that." She pushed a fry around. "But, hey, what are friends for?"

"Friends?" He'd never really been friends with a woman he hadn't grown up with, and he had a very select group of guys whom he was reasonably close to; that was just the way he liked to operate. The fewer deep connections the better.

She chuckled. "Yeah. You know, as in people who hang out and spend time together and talk to each other?"

"Oh. That," he said, ducking his head, playing along with her witty comeback, which seemed to break the ice even more.

That had to be why he felt the unusual need to confide in her. "Okay. Friends. Let's see." He cleared his throat. "The thing is, my childhood was a bit…tumultuous."

She leaned in. "How so?"

"My parents fought a lot," he admitted. "It kind of ruled our house, in a very chaotic way." As in nonstop fighting, 24/7.

"Oh, wow. That must have been hard," she said softly, her voice tinged with sympathy.

He relaxed a bit more as something eased inside of him. "Incredibly hard. They were always at odds—still are, actually—and I never really felt… at peace."

She nodded, a glow of understanding emanating from her eyes. "So now, I bet, you want lots of peace, don't you?" she asked, lifting up one delicate eyebrow.

His jaw went slack. She was very perceptive. Good or bad, he admired that trait. "Yeah. How did you know?"

She pressed her lips together. "Personal experience. I've had my share of chaos in my life, too."

"Oh, yeah. Your divorce. But you seem so well-adjusted and centered."

"It's all a well-crafted facade," she said flippantly, quirking a smile that didn't reach her eyes.

But he didn't believe her act. The flippancy was obviously hiding something. She'd been hurt. Deeply. And she was still hurting. His heart ached for her, but he wasn't sure what to say.

She confirmed his suspicions when she turned away, biting her lip. A few seconds later she looked back, tears glistening in her eyes. "In reality, I'm not well-adjusted at all."

Her tears kicked him in the gut. "Why?" he asked, oddly needing to know what made her tick.

She wiped away her tears. "My husband walked out on me and Dylan a year ago. My dad did the same thing to my mom and me when I was twelve."

His heart tipped, flooding him with more hurt on her behalf. Without thinking, he reached out and covered her hand with his own. "I'm sorry. They're idiots." Who would leave her and break her heart that way?

"Why do you say that?" she asked, her voice low and soft.

"Because they left an amazing person behind, and in the case of your ex, your great kid, too."

She turned her hand over and gripped his fingers, then reached out and put her free hand on his, rubbing lightly. She smiled shakily. "That's the nicest thing anyone's ever said to me."

Her warm, lingering touch made him feel like he'd been decked by a line drive. His breath was knocked out of him, along with his brains and good sense. "Well, it's true," he said.

She nodded as her tears welled and slipped down her face. He froze, staring at her wet cheeks. Oh, man. Full-fledged crying. Time to back off, keep the conversation more impersonal.

He pulled his hand away. He didn't want to get in too deep, right? So this wasn't a game he wanted to play.

No matter what the score.

Chapter Eight

To Kim, Seth looked as if he wanted to bolt.

Well, duh. Here she was, crying, opening up. Getting closer.

Sure, Seth was attractive. In many ways. But letting herself get drawn in to his appeal was unhealthy. Kind of like chocolate—you wanted a lot, but too much made you sorry.

She needed to keep her perspective and remember that analogy. She had to keep him at a distance to keep her heart whole and maintain her independence.

She looked out at the waves crashing on the shore. Would out there be far enough?

No, but Seattle would be.

"So," he said, drawing her attention again. "I doubt working retail in Moonlight Cove is your ultimate goal. What do you want to do with the rest of your life?"

"What's wrong with retail?" she asked, grateful for the change of subject. "You work in that area."

"True, but it's a family business, and as an owner, it does well as the only game in town."

"Good point," she replied. Earning minimum wage, then not much more for the rest of her life, would never help her meet her goals, much less support Dylan. "Actually, I want to get my teaching degree when I can afford college. I've been saving for years, and am close to being able to afford a term."

"A teacher." Seth nodded, his eyes reflecting what looked like approval. "Great goal."

His admiration warmed her, creating a warm glow inside to rival the sun setting over the ocean. "Thanks. I love working with kids, and would like to have the summers off to spend with Dyl."

"He's a great kid, you know."

A healthy dose of mother's pride filled her. "I appreciate the kudos." The breeze kicked up and she pushed her hair back from her face. "He's had a rough time since Scott left."

"I…imagine the breakup was hard on both of you," Seth said. "They usually are."

She focused on the kids playing in the park for a second. Would talking more about her split be smart? She glanced at Seth, drawn in by the understanding shining from his eyes. Maybe talking would be cathartic. "Yes, it was." Understatement. "Wait. Let me amend that. Why sugarcoat things? Starting over by myself was the hardest thing I've ever done."

"How did you manage? Rebounding from something like that is a tall order," he said softly, leaning his forearms on the picnic table.

Was that empathy she saw in his expression? "Sounds like you speak from experience."

"Hasn't everyone been dumped?" he said, cocking a brow.

She inclined her head to the side. "Probably." What was the story there? "The truth is, for a while I didn't manage. I was a mess. But then one day, I discovered something."

"What's that?" he asked, his face alight with an interest that, good or bad, she relished.

"I discovered that with the help of someone who loves me—my aunt—and my faith, I could deal with anything."

"Your faith?" he said.

"Well, yeah." She peered at him, surprised by his question. "God is a pretty good supporter when things get tough."

"Huh," Seth said, his eyes focused on the churning ocean for a moment, his brows pulled tight. Then his face smoothed. "I guess I've never really thought about Him in that way."

She sat up, taken aback by his statement. She

couldn't imagine not leaning on God. She took a swig of water, thinking. "Well, I have," she finally said, going for honesty. "God is always there, guiding me, supporting me, teaching me." A thought occurred to her. "Hey, you were at the church singles group the day you rescued me."

"True enough."

"So it seems like you must go to church, at least every once in a while."

"I do," he said, fiddling with his water bottle.

"But you don't understand my faith?" She pulled her jacket around her, feeling chilly. "What's up with that?"

He shrugged. "I go to church pretty often. In fact, I went to the pancake breakfast two Sundays ago. But during hard times, *depending* on my faith to get me through?" He frowned and shook his head. "I don't feel like God will help me."

She sat back, shocked. He was so different from her. They were miles apart, actually. "Why not?"

He looked out into the distance, staring at the ocean behind her. After a long moment he said, "Because I prayed for Him to make my parents stop fighting when I was younger, and the prayers didn't work."

"Oh, my," she said, blinking, suddenly understanding Seth so much better. He'd had it rough.

Really rough. "So now you've lost faith," she stated.

"Yeah, I have."

Intense sadness trailed through her. In her eyes, he was missing an important source of strength—God. "Well, I think you should give God another chance."

"That's really hard for me," he said, shifting. "I don't see the point."

Wow. He wasn't just *kind of* removed from God. He was light-years from rediscovering his faith.

Too many light-years, though? Could he be saved? "Okay. So you feel hopeless, you feel like God's abandoned you. But maybe if you established a deeper relationship with Him, your faith would grow stronger."

"I don't know how to do that," Seth said bluntly. "You care to explain?"

She sucked in a breath, thinking about how to put her connection to God into words. "For me, my commitment to God is so much more than just surface motions and social church activities. It's something that comes from within here," she said, putting her hand over her heart. "It's a deep connection that would be there even if I never set foot in a church again. It's a connection that is unwavering and visceral, and…"

"Intimate?" Seth filled in.

"Yes, exactly. It exists because of faith and trust

and the knowledge that everything is part of God's plan. He will be there for me, no matter what."

Seth sat quietly for a moment, clearly digesting what she'd said. "So how do you find this... connection?"

She pulled her thoughts together; she wanted to give him a good answer, wanted to verbalize to him what was important to her. Finally she said, "By trusting in God's power and wisdom and living your life in a way that will bring Him glory." She smiled gently, pleased. "And praying helps, too."

Seth gave her a rueful smile, and his eyes crinkled around the corners. "I have to say, I admire your level of spirituality."

"Thanks." She gazed at him for a moment. "You think you can find your faith again?"

"I don't know. Granted, you've made me wonder if I shouldn't seek a deeper connection to God. But I'm just not sure I'll be successful. *Losing faith* means just that. Losing faith, as in it's lost. Gone. I'm not certain I'll be able to ever hunt mine down, you know?"

"But that's the thing. Faith means hanging in there, even when the going gets tough. Trusting that things will get better no matter what, right? Faith begets faith."

He tilted his head to the side, obviously considering her words. "You make a good point, I'll give you that. But from my perspective, faith doesn't get me anywhere, so it's hard for me to hang in there."

Goodness, he was jaded—terribly so. That should be a warning to her. "The point is, you have to have faith to find faith."

"Exactly." His jaw tightened. "And I don't have any. So how can I find more?"

His words set her back. And broke her heart. How could someone live without trust in God? Without faith? She simply couldn't imagine such a thing.

A pit grew in her stomach. "Well, when you put it that way, I'm not sure what the answer is," she replied truthfully. "Seems like we're living on different planets, doesn't it?"

"Sure does," he said. "You live in one universe, and I live in another. What are the chances of them meeting?"

"Zero," she said after a moment. Everything he'd said was right on.

Why did that bother her?

Maybe…she needed to help Seth find faith. To help him reconnect with trusting God. Surely such a selfless undertaking couldn't be a bad thing.

But she halted the offer to help as it balanced on the tip of her tongue.

Chocolate, Kim. Remember chocolate.

Right. Helping him forge a deeper spiritual

connection was not the way to go about creating distance. Or fostering her own independence. No question. She'd just get drawn into something that wouldn't be good for her.

Regret poked at her, but she pushed the emotion away. *Help me, Lord, to be resolute.*

She didn't need Seth. She only needed herself.

He stared at her expectantly for a long moment, then yanked his gaze away and glanced at his watch. "Oh. Look at the time. We'd better get back to start on the inventory."

"Okay," she said, rising. Their discussion was over. Maybe that was a good thing; if there was ever a time to curb her impulsiveness, the moment was now, when she had so much at stake.

She helped him pick up the trash from their dinner, her hands shaking, her thoughts chaotic, despite her best efforts to stay on an even keel.

As they headed back to the store, she only hoped that she could keep her mind on the job. Because the sorry truth was that all she wanted to do was grab a huge bag of chocolate and eat the whole thing in one sitting.

Even if she paid the unavoidable price.

"Why don't I drive you home?" Seth said to Kim after they finished taking inventory around nine o'clock.

He'd have to thank his mom; due to her

orderliness, he and Kim had completed the counting chore in record time. Excellent. After his and Kim's heart-to-heart at the park, he was freaking out a bit. Too much closeness always made him uptight.

That said, he really admired her deep connection with God. But admiring something didn't make him think he'd ever have it. He was a realist, through and through. Had to be.

He would never share her faith.

Kim paused as she pulled on her hooded navy blue jacket. She looked at him, her eyes wide. "Um…no, thanks. I'd rather walk. I like—"

"The exercise and to reduce your carbon footprint," Seth supplied.

"You were listening," she replied, sounding kind of surprised he remembered. She'd told him when she arrived this morning that she preferred walking around town rather than driving whenever possible, both to keep in shape and to be greener. He liked her attempts to go green, actually. And obviously the in-shape part was working quite well.

"Why wouldn't I?" he asked, slightly puzzled by her comment.

"Oh, I don't know." She shrugged her slim shoulders. "Some people don't pay much attention."

"You have that right." His parents had been so busy being buried in conflict, attention for the kids had been slim while he'd been growing up. "Sometimes people get so caught up in their own problems, they don't pay attention to the ones they should."

"No kidding," she whispered, her pain clear, even though her words had been so soft he could barely hear them.

But he heard her. Loud and clear. She'd been wounded deeply by people in her life.

Why did he feel the need to heal that wound? Crazy.

Rattled, he stepped back. "I don't feel right letting you walk alone," he said softly, going back to the original subject of their conversation. He needed safer, more familiar ground. "Moonlight Cove is safe, but you never know. A gentleman doesn't let a lady walk around alone at night."

"Uh…that's sweet." She fumbled with the zipper on her hooded jacket. "But I can walk home by myself." She got the zipper to work and lifted her head. Her gorgeous brown eyes collided with his.

His breath left him in a rush. For a long second their gazes connected, blue to brown.

Sanity caught him. "No, no." He backed up. "I don't want you walking home by yourself. I'll get my jacket and we'll head out."

Kim tilted her head to one side. She hesitated

for another moment then said, "Okay. That'd be nice."

A few minutes later he'd locked up the store and they were headed toward Rose's house. The wind had died down, but the temperature had dropped to what Seth called "coastal cool." It was a beautiful summer evening, with clear skies, sparkling stars and, appropriately, a glowing moon hanging low in the darkening, orange-tinted sky.

There were still plenty of people on the boardwalk, many of them families congregated around I Scream for Ice Cream, a popular shop on Main Street owned by his best friend Drew's sister, Phoebe Sellers.

The scent of waffle cones drifted on the air, and Seth's mouth watered. "You want some ice cream?" he asked as they approached the brightly lit store. "I know the owner and could probably swing a deal."

Kim put her hands into her jacket pockets, and he had to fight the urge to fish out the hand nearest him and put it in his own pocket.

She hesitated, biting her lip, then craned her gaze to look into the festively decorated ice cream parlor. "Actually, that sounds good."

"Great." He went over and opened the door. "After you."

With a small smile that made his heart tilt, she preceded him in. As they waited in line, kids ran around and peered into the giant, glass-topped coolers lining two walls of the store.

"My aunt has a weakness for ice cream," Kim said. "She and Dylan come here a lot."

"I have a weakness for it, too," Seth said. Along with a weakness for pretty brown eyes. Not that he was thinking about that.

"What's your favorite?" she asked.

"Coffee." He ripped his eyes from her and craned his head to see in the ice cream case. "What's yours? I bet you're a praline pecan girl, aren't you?"

"Oh, no," she said. "My favorite is chocolate."

"Hmm. Just plain chocolate?"

"Yup. Give me a big scoop of that, and I'm a happy camper."

"Obviously, you're a no-nonsense kind of gal." He got out his wallet. "Good for you."

An attractive blush spread across her cheeks. "Thanks."

They made it to the front of the line and ordered.

While they waited for their cones, Phoebe, the owner, stepped out from the back of the store. She had her long, curly blond hair piled on top of her head and wore a black T-shirt with the words *I Scream* emblazoned across the front in hot pink letters. As always, she looked much younger than her actual age of thirty.

"Hey, Seth," she said, wiping her hands on a towel. "How're you doing?"

Seth waved. "Good, Phoebs." He gestured to Kim. "This is Kim Hampton. Kim, this is Phoebe Sellers."

Phoebe beamed, her cornflower blue eyes darting speculatively between him and Kim. She reached out to shake Kim's hand. "Pleased to meet you."

"Pleased to meet you, too," Kim said, taking Phoebe's hand.

Phoebe shoved the towel in the back pocket of her jeans. "Hey, I heard how you rescued her the other day."

"Yeah, it was nothing," Seth said. He went over and took their cones from the teenager behind the counter.

"Those are on the house, by the way," Phoebe said, nodding toward their ice cream. "And call me silly, but I think saving Kim's life is something." She gave him a mildly scolding look. "And I'm sure Kim agrees."

"Definitely," Kim said, laughing. "And my son does, too."

"Oh, yeah," Phoebe said, nodding. "He comes in all the time with Rose, doesn't he?"

"Blond kid, dripping in strawberry ice cream?" Kim said. "That'd be him."

"Yup," said Phoebe. Phoebe caught Seth's gaze.

"Drew told me that he really had to cajole you into going to the singles group bonfire. Aren't you glad you went now? If you hadn't, who would have saved Kim?"

Her point wasn't lost on Seth; he'd thought the same thing the day he'd rescued Kim. "Your brother has always encouraged me to be more social." Especially around people they hadn't grown up with.

Forming new relationships had been difficult for Seth; he was much more comfortable around his childhood friends like Drew, Lily and Phoebe. He took comfort in the familiar. "Guess it's a good thing I caved and went to the bonfire, isn't it?"

"Sure is," Phoebe replied with a knowing look. No surprise she agreed with Drew's tactics. Like sister, like brother. "Remember that the next time you want to hole up in your house by yourself." She pointed at him. "Someone might need rescuing."

He whistled. "She's tough, isn't she?" he said to Kim.

"That, and she clearly has your best interests at heart," Kim replied. "Sounds like you have some true friends."

"The best," he said, realizing then that there were some good things that came from close relationships.

Maybe he should consider expanding his circle.

To include Kim?

Phoebe's eyes went to the front of the store and widened. "Uh-oh. Ice cream droppage by the door. Better go." She looked at Kim. "Good to meet you."

"You, too," Kim replied.

They said goodbye to Phoebe, left the store and were soon walking down the boardwalk, on their way toward Rose's cottage five blocks north of Main Street.

A block into their journey, Seth glanced west. "Let's walk on the beach," he suggested between licks of coffee bliss. "Maybe we can see the moon on the water. No one should miss that." One of his favorite sights, for sure. Wordlessly she agreed and made a left in sync with him.

As expected, the silvery moon hung low in the sky, lighting the way. He walked silently next to Kim. She was quiet, too, seemingly lost in her own thoughts, whatever they were.

Despite his best efforts to rein it in, his curiosity about her faith grew. "I've been thinking a lot about what you said at the park." He polished off his ice cream, then glanced her way.

She put the last bit of her cone into her mouth and chewed. "Which part?" she asked when she was finished.

"All of it," he said truthfully as they reached the

ocean's edge. "But the part about your faith really stuck with me."

She stopped, gazing out at the water, her lovely sculpted face profiled against the dusky gray, rust and dark blue streaked horizon. "How so?"

He stepped toward her. "I was struck by how close you are to God, and how it comes from here," he said, gesturing to his heart. "But in reality, I've been thinking I won't ever have that connection."

She turned and regarded him, her gaze questioning. "I know you said that. But I still think faith comes with faith, and that with one, you'll find the other. But you have to believe to begin with, you know?"

He lifted one shoulder. "On one level, I agree with you. But on another, I wasn't raised to have an intimate, truly meaningful relationship with God."

She nodded. "I understand. But you have to believe from the start. As long as you don't...well, then, you're right. Growing closer to God won't happen."

"I get what you're saying," he said. "But what you're suggesting seems a tad idealistic to the realist in me."

She skewered him with a steady gaze. "True, because God is definitely an idealist. That's the beauty of His grace."

Before he could reply, he spied a sneaker wave rolling in, fast.

"Hey!" he exclaimed, pulling on her hand and running backward, out of the water's reach. "Watch out!"

She squealed and ran with him to safety. The water just missed soaking their feet.

"Whoa." She danced back another few steps. "That was a fast one."

He swung her to him and said, "Gotta watch out for those." Man, he liked being close to her.

"Thanks for saving me," she said, turning in toward him. She gazed up at him, her face near again. The moon shining down touched her cheeks in silver, highlighting her perfect bone structure with various shades of blue and gray. "You seem to be my rescuer."

"You're worth saving," he said, meaning the words, even though the sentiment took him off guard in a huge way.

She gave him a tremulous smile. "Thank you. That means a lot."

Her words reminded him of how much hurt she'd had in her life. Both her ex and her dad had deserted her. But she'd survived and moved on.

His heart pounded, mixing with the crash of the ocean in the background. Seth put his other arm around her. He dipped his head, drawn to the strong, resilient woman she was shaping up to be in a way he couldn't seem to effectively fight. She met him halfway, and he pressed his lips to hers.

She tasted like sugar and chocolate…

And an unmistakable connection.

Warning bells went off in his head and he forced himself to pull away. He was headed for foul territory. No doubt about it. Time to back off and let Kim go.

Wasn't that what he always did?

Chapter Nine

Shaking, Kim stepped even farther away from Seth, pressing her fingers to her lips. "That was a mistake," she said. A big one. Huge.

Why was she letting Seth kiss her, anyway? Why wasn't she able to think straight?

Seth wasn't the type to settle down. He had no faith. She wasn't planning on staying in town. Letting her guard falter would only hurt her and Dylan in the end. She had to stay solitary, or risk pain. She'd learned that lesson well in the past. A few times.

Seth looked at the sand and readjusted his hat. "Yes, it was."

See. He agreed with her. She needed to be smart and strong. Needed to reinforce the wall around her heart, the one that was having a hard time resisting this man. "Um, I think I better get home then."

He swiped a hand over his shadowed jaw, then swept a hand in the direction of Aunt Rose's house. "Shall we?" His voice held an edge she'd never heard before, an edge that made her chest tighten painfully.

This was a wake-up call. She would not let another man have the power to hurt her. She wanted to depend only on herself from now on. For her happiness, her life, her goals.

"We shall," she said, raising her chin. She shoved her hands into her jacket pockets, telling herself to be smart. Cautious.

The wind kicked up, making her eyes burn as she started heading back to the wet, more solid sand closer to the ocean for the short walk to Aunt Rose's house. Seth followed a ways back, silent, giving—and taking—space.

Good for him. She needed to follow suit.

Because if she didn't discover a way to get on a more even keel with Seth—fast—she had a big, big problem on her hands.

When Kim got home, after she and Seth exchanged good-nights, she paused for a second on the porch and pressed cool hands to her warm cheeks, getting herself under control after her and Seth's mistaken but wonderful kiss on the beach.

Better.

A bit more centered, she went into the house and found Aunt Rose and Benny sitting at the dining room table doing a jigsaw puzzle.

They had their two gray heads bent over the table, and both of them had their glasses propped up on their heads as they scanned the puzzle pieces.

Kim paused and gazed at the quaint scene, not that surprised to see Benny hanging out with Rose. He'd been around more and more lately, often under the guise of Dylan interacting with the puppies. But now, though…here he was, with no puppies around, and Dylan was in bed. Benny and Rose were alone.

Interesting.

"Hey, you two," Kim said, waving.

They both looked up.

"Hello, dear," Aunt Rose replied, sliding her glasses down onto her nose.

Benny followed suit with his spectacles. "Hi, Kim."

Kim moved farther into the room, scanning the huge amount of puzzle pieces spread out across the table. "That looks like a hard one." Probably a whole week's worth of evenings spent together, actually. Looked like her aunt and her would-be suitor might be spending a lot of time with each other.

Again, interesting.

"Benny's promised me this one's doable, although I'm not so sure." Rose smiled fondly and patted his arm. "Haven't you?"

Benny blushed and nodded, staring at the place on his arm Rose had touched. He swallowed, then readjusted his wire-rimmed glasses. "Uh...yeah," he stammered. "I...I've done a lot of these." As usual, he had trouble speaking when Rose was around.

Crush, for sure, just as Kim had thought.

Kim smiled inwardly, then sat down and helped find edge pieces for a while, enjoying the quiet task after being so thrown by kissing Seth on the beach.

As Kim worked on the puzzle with Rose and Benny, she noted how happy the older pair seemed to be spending these ordinary moments together. They made a darling couple, her aunt fair and small, Benny dark and tall. They looked as if they belonged together.

She was sure her aunt would disagree.

At one point, Kim saw Benny sending a few longing looks toward Rose, which, deep down, made Kim yearn for someone of her own. But her practical side pushed such dangerous thoughts away, and instead she concentrated on putting one long edge of the puzzle together. She'd had enough emotional drama for one night. Maybe for a lifetime.

Kissing Seth had definitely put her into a funk.

Finally, Rose's grandfather clock in the living room bonged the hour. Benny looked at his watch. "Oh, it's getting late." He stood, running a hand through his still-thick gray hair. "I'd better go let the mama and her pups out."

Kim got to her feet. "Good to see you, Benny."

He nodded, smiling. "You, too. Be sure and let Dylan know he's welcome at my house any time."

Kim guessed Rose would be very welcome, too. "I'll tell him."

Rose walked to the front door with Benny. Kim heard their murmured voices saying goodbye in the entryway, and a moment later, Rose came back into the dining room. "Did you walk home all alone, dear?" she asked Kim.

Kim concentrated on looking for the last edge puzzle piece. "No. Seth walked me here." No use hiding the truth. Why would she want to, anyway?

Aunt Rose didn't respond.

Kim looked up questioningly after a few beats of silence, noting the lines forming on Rose's forehead. "Is there something on your mind?" she asked.

Rose sat down. "I may be out of line with this, but I just thought I should warn you about Seth."

Kim frowned. *"Warn me?"* She couldn't have been more surprised if her aunt had pulled out of her pocket a polka-dotted snake wearing a top hat. "What, is he a criminal or something?"

Rose shook her head. "No, no. Of course not. Seth is a successful and respected businessman in town." She reached out and put a firm hand on Kim's. "But, unfortunately, he's a…" her voice dropped to a whisper "…hound dog."

Kim stared at her aunt for a moment. "Hound dog?" She scrunched up her face. "What, exactly, do you mean?"

Rose let go of Kim's hand and pressed her lips together. "Well, my dear, it's a well-known fact around here that Seth is a bit of a playboy."

Kim sat back, staring at her aunt. Echoes of what Elwood had said reverberated through her mind. *"A playboy?"* Kim had visions of a Hugh Hefner type, sitting around in a satin smoking jacket. That didn't sound like Seth at all.

Aunt Rose nodded sagely. "Yes, indeed. He's dated every unmarried woman in town, but he doesn't seem inclined to settle down."

"Every one?" Kim said, raising an eyebrow. "That's a lot of women." Maybe levity would make this somewhat familiar conversation less disconcerting. Maybe not.

Rose shrugged. "Every gal under the age of thirty." She pulled her glasses off her head and laid them down on the table. "Well, maybe thirty-five. He dated Luanne Keller last summer, and she tells everyone she's twenty-nine." She scoffed. "But she's thirty-five if she's a day."

"Ah, I see." Kim laughed nervously. "Well, that narrows it down. And you're telling me this because…?" She trailed off so her aunt could make her point. Explain. If that was remotely possible. Why did everyone feel the need to fill her in on Seth's dating past?

Rose sighed. "We've already talked about how you don't want to get hurt by love again, right?"

"Right," Kim said. So she definitely shouldn't be kissing Seth anymore. Not exactly a news flash, but duly noted and acknowledged. Again. Especially now that Rose had reinforced what Elwood had told Kim.

"So, a girl being careful with her heart should know these things," Rose said with a knowing nod.

Kim studied the puzzle pieces for a long moment, formulating her thoughts. Obviously she needed to put her aunt's mind at ease about falling for her appealing boss. And her own mind, too, for that matter.

Maybe verbalizing would help Kim reiterate the need to keep Seth at arm's length, for both her sake and Dylan's. The last thing she wanted was for her son to become attached to Seth. She had a feeling there was only disappointment down that road; Scott had taught her that lesson well.

Her gaze snagged on the puzzle piece she'd been hunting for. She picked it up. "I appreciate your warning, Aunt Rose, but there's nothing to worry about. I'm not going to be getting involved with Seth." Kim meant the words, truly she did. And she certainly wouldn't be kissing him again.

With a flourish, she snapped the piece into place, completing the edge of the puzzle. She carefully adjusted the puzzle's border until it was perfectly square, perfectly tidy, perfectly done and ready for the rest of the picture to be completed.

Unbidden, memories of the kiss she'd shared with Seth flashed through her mind, filling her all over again with an unwanted yearning for something more in her life.

Something she could never allow herself to have.

And she could only hope that the dilemma of her risky attraction to Seth versus her need to remain independent—and to protect Dylan—would be solved as neatly as the puzzle on the table before her.

God, I hope you're listening.

Chapter Ten

Two days after he'd kissed Kim on the beach, Seth stepped back and took a look at his handiwork in the men's footwear display.

He saw Kim in the middle of aisle three out of the corner of his eye. Shifting his gaze a bit, he surreptitiously watched her for a second. She wore a well-fitting pair of dark blue jeans, a lime green, short-sleeve top and her work apron. How did one woman manage to make casual clothes look so good?

And their kiss? He wouldn't be forgetting that anytime soon.

She wandered over, scanning the display he'd just spent an hour rearranging, an eyebrow raised.

"What do you think?" he asked her.

"Looks…great, I guess. So, now the men's shoes are arranged from largest to smallest." She gestured at the display, her head cocked at an angle. "Horizontally?"

He nodded. "Yup. This setup is much more intuitive for the customers, don't you think?"

"Um…sure. Whatever you say," she said, her lip quivering as if she was holding back a smile. "Listen. Is it okay if I take my lunch now? I need to run to the pharmacy to get some stuff."

"Sure. Take as much time as you need."

"Thanks." He watched her grab her purse from behind the counter and head outside, the bells over the door ringing when she left.

He turned back to survey his work again, seeing it through Kim's eyes. Had he really just spent an hour on this ridiculous project? Was he finding excuses to be out in the store, doing busy work to be around her?

Nah. He enjoyed this kind of merchandising stuff. Right? He'd be sure and do more of it once his mom came back to work. No question. Besides, Kim had shown him that maybe the store did need a little rearranging here and there.

And kissing Kim? As Kim had said—a mistake. A moment of weakness.

A young boy's voice interrupted his thoughts. "Hey, Mr. Graham. How're you doing?"

Seth spun around, surprised to find Dylan Hampton standing in the middle of the store, waving. He was dressed for baseball practice, his brand-spanking-new glove dangling from his small hand.

"Hey, Dylan. I didn't hear you come in."

"Mom had just left." He smiled, showing the gap between his front teeth. "The door closes slow."

Seth glanced around. "Are you here alone?"

"Nope, Auntie Rose is outside, talking to her friend." He gestured with his chin toward the front windows. "We're running errands."

Seth saw Rose outside, talking to Virginia Crane. "Oh. Good. What can I do for you?"

Dylan moved closer. "Well, I found out my baseball coach had to go on a trip." He scrunched up his face, his freckled nose wrinkling. "He's gotta work."

"Oh, no. That's too bad." Seth's skin prickled.

"Yeah. So, I was wondering…" Dylan turned his big blue eyes up to Seth. "Can you coach us while he's gone?"

Seth tried to picture where his car keys were to make a quick escape. Coaching was public and personal at the same time…

"Please?" Dylan said, his face pleading. "Today is supposed to be our first practice, and if we don't get a coach, it isn't gonna happen." He held up his gloved hand. "I've got my glove all ready, too."

Seth thought back to his first baseball practice. He'd worn his baseball clothes all day long, barely able to wait until it was time to go to the ball field.

He would have been devastated if practice had been canceled. Absolutely devastated.

He eyed Dylan. "What time is practice? Now? Because now would be out of the question with the store to run and all."

"Not until six."

Seth snagged a glance at his watch. It was two o'clock. Looked like Dylan had been dressed and ready for a good part of the day. Sounded familiar.

"Six?" he asked, wavering.

Dylan nodded, his eyes wide. "Please, please, please? I'll sweep the whole store."

Seth took a deep breath, feeling his reluctance cave in the face of Dylan's eagerness and enthusiasm for a game Seth loved. Really, coaching might be fun; after all, baseball was his forte, his passion, the safe place he'd gone as a kid to escape the chaos of his parents' home. The one place he could be in control.

Besides, the moms just dropped the kids off, then left. He wouldn't be forming any new adult relationships, would he? Somehow, he felt more comfortable interacting with Dylan. He'd probably enjoy the time spent with some rowdy boys, too. He'd been one once.

He reached out and plucked Dylan's baseball cap off and plopped the too-small hat on his own head. "Okay. I'll coach. Where do we meet?"

Dylan jumped up and down. "Moonlight Cove Elementary School."

"See you there."

A huge smile lit Dylan's face. "Thanks, Mr. Graham. You're the best. I'm going to go tell Auntie Rose the good news."

Seth took the cap off his own head and held it out. "Don't forget this."

Dylan ran back and grabbed the hat out of Seth's hand. "Oh, yeah."

Grinning, Seth watched Dylan run off and out the front door. The boy's zeal was contagious. Coaching would be a lot of fun; surprisingly, Seth really relished the opportunity to pass along his love and knowledge of America's pastime to kids. The baseball diamond was his stomping ground.

A thought dug at him, though. What would Kim think of this baseball coaching arrangement? She'd been reluctant for him to spend time with Dylan so far. Belatedly he realized that she might not be happy at all about him coaching Dylan's team.

Seth guessed he would have to deal with that as best he could. What was done was done, and he never went back on his word.

As Kim walked back to The Sports Shack from the pharmacy, enjoying the sunny day, she spied Dylan and Aunt Rose walking up the boardwalk half a block away.

They must be out running errands.

Dylan was already dressed for baseball practice, even though he knew that the coach was out of town and that having a full-on practice was iffy unless a parent with some baseball knowledge stepped forward to act as temporary head coach. Kim was happy to assist at games, but she wasn't comfortable enough with the ins and outs of the game to coach full-time.

Apparently hope dwelled eternal in a baseball-crazy kid's mind, though; Dylan obviously was expecting something to work out in the coaching department. She prayed her son wouldn't be too disappointed if practice had to be postponed. If nothing else, maybe she could at least get the boys on the team together for a game of catch or something.

A few moments later, Dylan spotted her and his face lit up. He ran the rest of the distance between them, leaving Rose to bring up the rear.

"Guess what, Mom?" he announced, words flying from his mouth even before he'd reached her.

"What?" Goodness, he seemed excited.

"Mr. Graham is going to coach my team!" Dylan crowed, jumping up and down in enthusiasm.

Her stomach fell. "How did that happen?"

Dylan puffed out his chest. "I asked him just now, and he said yes!"

"He did?" She wished Seth had checked with her before agreeing.

"Yup. He's gonna be at the field at six."

Kim chewed on her lip. This was disconcerting news; how could she guard against Dylan becoming attached to Seth if they spent time together this way?

Aunt Rose walked up. "Hello, dear." She held up a plastic bag. "We were just on our way to the cobbler to get my shoes repaired."

Kim nodded distractedly. "I could have dropped those off for you."

"Nonsense," Aunt Rose said, waving a hand in the air. "We need the exercise, and I promised Dylan a trip to the park on the way home." She patted his back. "He couldn't wait to get down here."

I'll bet, Kim thought. He'd probably been anxious to waylay Seth into coaching. "A trip to the park sounds great," Kim replied, hiding her dismay about the coaching situation with an even tone.

As much as she didn't really like Seth coaching Dylan's team, she wouldn't dream of making Dylan feel bad for asking. He'd been looking forward to the first practice for days.

"Bye, Mom," Dylan said, his voice bright and cheery. "You're coming to practice, right?"

"You bet, sweetie. I'll swing by the house after work and pick you up."

"I can't wait!" he said, tugging on Rose's hand. "Mr. Graham is gonna be the best coach ever!"

Rose adjusted her sun hat, then gave Kim a significant look. Her earlier warning about Seth echoed in Kim's head.

"Did you know Dylan talked Seth into coaching?" she asked Rose conversationally, her eyebrows arched high.

Rose blinked. "No, I didn't know," she said after a pause, her voice going up an octave. "That should be...fun."

Kim shook her head ever so slightly, then said, "Yes, just what I was thinking." Meaning not so much.

Rose gave her a knowing look, obviously understanding Kim's "code," then she slanted a glance at Dylan and pursed her lips. She mouthed "I'm sorry."

Kim mouthed "no problem" back. No sense in getting Rose upset about what had happened. It was Kim's problem, not her aunt's, and Dylan was a hard kid to keep from what he wanted.

"I'll have sandwiches ready so you guys can eat before you leave." Rose looked at Dylan. "I'll make potato salad, too, young man."

"Yum!" Dylan replied, his blue eyes bright. "I love your potato salad."

Rose's mouth turned up at the corners. "I know, silly. That's why I'm going to make it."

"That sounds wonderful," Kim said. What would she do without Aunt Rose once they moved to Seattle? Being alone would be hard, although she'd have her cousin, Grant, to help out once in a while. "Thank you. Have fun, and I'll see you two later. I have to get back to work." She'd need to have a word with Seth when she arrived; what had he been thinking?

Rose took Dylan by the hand, and they headed in the direction of the park. Kim watched them for a block or so, her brow furrowed. Dylan broke free from Rose and skipped ahead, a distinct bounce in his step, clearly thrilled by the turn of events.

Kim had to give the little guy some credit. He'd enlisted a former baseball player to coach his team. Dylan had a bad case of hero worship going on and it was probably his dream come true to have Seth help out, if only for a little while.

Too bad she wasn't as thrilled. She had to protect her son from being hurt when another male figure walked out and broke his heart.

Time to have a talk with Seth. No matter how much she wasn't looking forward to the task.

After Dylan left, Seth went back to work in the footwear section, setting his mind on rearranging the hiking boot display to keep busy.

A few minutes later, the bells over the door rang. Seth glanced up, a shoe box in his hand.

Kim walked to the front counter and put her purse down, then headed straight to the back of the store, her mouth tight. Seth braced himself for the coming storm.

"I just saw Dylan," she said.

Might as well get straight to the point. "So you know I'm coaching tonight."

She nodded stiffly. "Why didn't you talk with me about this first?"

"Honestly, it didn't even occur to me." He put the box down. "All I could think about was that I didn't want Dylan to be disappointed."

"Oh."

"I should have checked with you, I guess, before I committed. But I remembered how excited I was for my first baseball practice, and I couldn't say no."

She pressed a hand to her heart, sighing. "I appreciate that, I really do. I just wish you had talked to me before you agreed."

"It's one practice. We can even cut it short if that would make you feel better."

"Actually, I talked to the coach earlier today. He's on an emergency business trip for a week. That means three practices and a game next Saturday. You up for something along those lines?"

A week's worth of practices. Not just one. And a game…

"Sure," he said, trying to sound as if coaching

little kids was a piece of cake, when…well, he wasn't so sure. "I made a promise. I'm not going to back out now. A million practices, whatever. As long as Dylan isn't let down."

She pursed her glossy lips. "You're a stand-up guy, aren't you?"

"I try to be." Even though he hadn't had particularly good role models growing up, at least at home. Luckily, he'd had a couple really good baseball coaches who'd had a positive impact on him and, now that he thought about it, made him want to do the same for Dylan's team.

"Well, you're succeeding."

Her compliment pleased him. Maybe more than it should. "Thanks."

"The thing is…do you know who the assistant coach is?" she asked softly.

"Not a clue."

"Yours truly," she said, quirking a nervous smile.

He blinked. "I had no way of knowing that, obviously. If that's a problem for you, I'm sure I can coach the team on my own. I happen to be very good at baseball. I don't really need an assistant. You're off the hook."

"Not what I meant," she said, holding up both of her index fingers in the air. "I'll help out for sure."

He frowned. "Why are you so intent on being the assistant?"

She sighed and looked at the ceiling for a moment. "To tell you the truth, I want to be sure Dylan doesn't get too attached to you."

Offense sizzled through Seth, even though he knew she had trust issues concerning Dylan. "Because I'm such a bad influence? Gce, thanks."

"Oh, no, no. That's not it," she said, sounding sincere. "I just don't want him to…suffer any emotional pain."

The fact that she thought he would hurt Dylan dug its way under Seth's skin. "So you think I'm going to become friends with your son, then hurt him?"

"Not intentionally," she said. "But ever since Scott walked out on Dylan, I've been extra protective. He's been hurt once by an adult letting him down. I don't want him to be hurt again."

Seth stared at her, his chest tight with an ache he didn't understand. She was right; Dylan had been hurt by his dad, and Seth certainly knew how painful a father failing his son could be.

Still, it didn't feel good to be lumped in with her ex-husband. Not good at all.

"All right. I can see why you'd be concerned," he said honestly. He picked up a hiking boot box, opened it and rearranged the footwear inside. "All I can say is that I promise I won't hurt your son." She was just trying to do the right thing for her child; how could he fault her for her stance? He only wished his parents had been as concerned with their kids' well-being when Seth and his brothers were growing up.

She raised her chin. "I'm going to hold you to that promise."

"I'll keep my word." And he would. The last thing he wanted to do was emulate his father and let down the kids in his life.

"I hope you do. My number one concern is Dylan."

A warm glow of appreciation spread through him. She was a mother protecting her cub. "I expect nothing less from you. You're a good mom."

"Well, thanks." She headed toward the front of the store, then stopped and turned. "The baseball coach die has been cast, so we'll just have to deal. But so you know, I'm only going along with this coaching thing because you've already promised Dylan, all right?"

"All right," Seth told her, trying to sound as if her words didn't slash into him. What else was there to say? Nothing. Absolutely nothing. He was only her son's temporary coach.

Great. Perfect. Wonderful.

So why did her declaration make him feel so empty inside?

Chapter Eleven

A half hour into baseball practice, Kim stood in the dugout with the team, looking around the field through the metal backstop in front of the bench.

She saw one boy plucking dandelions from the outfield, another kicking up the dirt of the infield and a third climbing like a monkey on the lower part of the backstop not three feet from her.

What had she and Seth gotten themselves into?

Nothing like trying to get twelve seven-year-olds to focus. On anything. But Seth being coach was good for the kids. Sure. He was perfect for the job, actually.

Had she overreacted earlier?

"Brandon, you're running the wrong way," Seth said from the pitcher's mound. He pointed left. "That way."

Brandon, the batter, ran in a circle, and then headed off toward first base—cutting right across the infield.

Seth smiled crookedly, then looked at Kim, shrugging casually. "Remind me to work on the running pattern later."

A flitter of attraction darted around in her. No wonder women liked him. She cleared her throat. "Okay," she said, the words *hound dog* reverberating in her brain.

"Yo, Jordan," Seth called to the redheaded kid on the backstop. "You're up. Andrew, you're in the hole."

Jordan froze. "I don't wanna bat," he said. "I'll just watch."

With an athlete's grace, Seth jogged to home base, then approached Jordan from the opposite side of the backstop. "Why not, Spider-Man?"

"I'm afraid of the ball," Jordan replied. "It hurts when it hits you."

Seth eyed him. "You look pretty brave, though."

"I do?"

"Yeah, look at you, climbing all over the place." Seth gestured to the backstop. "Aren't you afraid you'll fall?"

"Nah. I do this all the time."

"So you've had practice, right?" Seth asked,

adjusting his baseball cap, his smaller Band-Aid flashing.

Jordan nodded.

"Well, then, don't you think you should practice hitting the ball so you won't be scared of it?"

Good angle, Kim thought.

"Yeah. I guess," Jordan admitted.

Seth rounded the backstop, then reached up and plucked Jordan down. "Can I share a secret with you?" he mock-whispered in Jordan's ear.

Jordan nodded, his eyes widening.

"I was afraid of the ball when I was your age, too."

"No way," Jordan said. "Pros are never afraid of the ball."

Seth put Jordan down. "I didn't start out as a pro, though. And when I was your age, I flinched every time the pitcher threw the ball in my direction."

Jordan squished his eyebrows together. "What'd you do?"

Seth squatted down so he was eye level with Jordan. "I imagined the ball was made out of foam."

Jordan squinted at Seth. "Like a NERF ball?"

"Sure. Like that," Seth said. "Works every time."

"Really?"

"Yup. You wanna try my trick and see how

it goes?" Seth rose and pointed to the pitcher's mound. "I can move in a bit if you want."

"O-okay," Jordan said. "I'll try."

Seth patted him on the shoulder, then bent down and picked up the nearest batting helmet. "Good attitude, Jordan. All I ask is that you try." He handed the helmet to Jordan. "Let's go bat some NERF balls."

With a lump in her throat, Kim watched Seth go out until he was standing about fifteen feet from the batter's box. Jordan put on the helmet, then gingerly picked up the bat and got into position.

"Now," Seth said gently. "I'm going to pitch from here, real easy, all right?"

"'Kay," Jordan said, his voice filled with apprehension.

Seth pitched the ball very slowly, and Jordan jumped back with a squeak, his eyes squeezed shut.

"No problem," Seth said a moment later. "Now you know where I'm going to put it, right?"

Jordan nodded. "Right."

Once Seth had the ball again, he held it up. "NERF, remember?"

"Okay," Jordan replied.

"And try to keep your eyes open this time, or you'll never see where the ball is," Seth instructed. He looked at Kim and winked.

Seth pitched again, and, miraculously, Jordan

actually got a piece of the ball—a weak grounder, yes, but it was enough of a hit that it bounced and rolled right by Seth, who made a weak attempt to stop the ball.

Jordan let out a hoot and dropped the bat, then started running toward first base, his short legs pumping for all they were worth.

The other boys in the dugout with Kim cheered him on. Seth grabbed the ball and threw it to the first baseman, Wyatt, trying for the out. But little Wyatt had his eyes trained away from the field— probably daydreaming—and he was clearly bliss-fully unaware the ball had even been thrown his way.

The ball bounced in the dirt not five feet from Wyatt, and then rolled into foul territory and stopped dead.

A second later, Jordan was safe. The man on first made it to second. And Dylan made it from third to home.

Everybody cheered, including Kim. She hugged Dylan, then looked up and saw Seth walk over to talk to Wyatt, who was now hanging his head; he'd obviously tuned back into the practice and was aware of his mistake.

"Don't worry about it," Seth called as he made his way to first base. When he reached Wyatt, he hunkered down, a gentle hand on Wyatt's small shoulder, his large body dwarfing the boy.

Kim observed Seth speak softly, earnestly, to Wyatt. She couldn't hear the exact words, but she could discern Seth was trying to soothe Wyatt's distress over missing the play.

Seth reached out and lifted Wyatt's chin. He said something else, then stood, nodding. Wyatt nodded back, and then, with Seth's hand still on Wyatt's shoulder, they both began to walk to the dugout. Wyatt had a tentative smile on his face.

Kim watched them approach the rest of the team, the big man and the small boy, her heart contracting.

"I've got juice in that cooler over there." Kim pointed to a large blue cooler in the grass. "Why doesn't everybody take a break, okay?" She needed one.

The boys ran toward the ice chest.

With his glove hanging from his left hand, Seth approached. His eyes glowed blue in his face against the backdrop of the summer evening sky.

She fought the urge to stare; he was just so handsome. And nice to the kids. Instead of looking at him, she adjusted her baseball cap, cutting off the seemingly endless list of Seth's admirable traits. "That was a nice thing you did out there."

He picked up the water bottle he'd brought with him. "What did I do?"

"You let Jordan's hit go right by you."

"What makes you think that?" He popped open the bottle and took a swig of water.

"Oh, come on," she said, propping her hands on her hips. "You're in great, um…shape, and the hit was a grounder that wasn't exactly going at the speed of light."

He lifted one broad shoulder. "It was a good hit, and I'm not as fast as I used to be," he said, gesturing to his right knee. "Bum knee."

"Yeah, right." She liked what he'd done for Jordan. But she liked even more that Seth wasn't looking for accolades; she could see all he really wanted was to be a positive influence on the kids. So all she said was, "You're quite a coach, Mr. Graham. I'm impressed."

Was he actually blushing?

"Well, that means a lot, Ms. Hampton." He homed in on her eyes and held her gaze. "Especially coming from you."

She couldn't look away. Could barely even breathe.

Seth held up his water bottle once again, guzzled the liquid and set it back on the bench. As he headed over to the boys' watering hole, he clapped his hands. "All right, guys," he shouted. "Let's get back out on the field and go over how to run the bases."

Kim swallowed and watched him go, pressing trembling hands to her warm face. Seeing the good man in Seth was becoming perilous territory indeed.

Chapter Twelve

"So, it seems like you've made a miraculous recovery," Seth said to his mom when she arrived bright and early at work two days after the first baseball practice.

She looked the picture of good health in her stylish pair of jeans and short-sleeve green shirt embroidered with The Sports Shack's logo. Her short blond hair was, as usual, perfectly styled.

As she headed around the front counter, she froze, seeming to remember her "sick" story.

Dramatically coughing into her elbow, she said, "I'm still a bit under the weather." Clearly she'd roughed up her voice intentionally. "But you told me when you called last night that it's Kim's day off, so what choice did I have but to fill in, despite my illness?"

Seth put his hands on his hips and scoffed. "Oh,

come on, Mom. Cut the act. You know you've been faking ever since you got back from Seattle."

She paused, her chin tilted up, obviously considering her response options. To give in, or keep up the act? Which way would she go?

To say that his mom was unpredictable was an understatement. Her way of keeping her family off balance?

Boy, had her ploy worked.

Finally, she inclined her head in a concessional way. "Okay, you've got me there."

Surprise bounced through him. She didn't usually give up so easily. "You bet I do. You're not that good of an actress."

"You went along with my story, though, didn't you?" she asked, a brow arched slyly. "You didn't put up much of an argument."

"What choice did I have?" he asked, spreading his arms wide. "You're stubborn. We both know there's no changing your mind once you decide to do something."

"Or maybe you bought my story because, deep down, you wanted to work with Kim," she said softly but confidently, leaning on the counter, her light blue gaze drilling into him with the accuracy of one of his dad's hunting rifles. "Did you ever think of that?"

He flinched inwardly. Okay. Direct hit. She was playing hardball now, of course. She always did.

Bring it on. He needed to set her straight about his feelings for Kim. "I never believed your story, Mom."

"I know. But you *agreed* to it, didn't you?" She straightened, then shrugged. "That's what matters, dear."

Unease trickled through him. "Means nothing," he said quickly, automatically. Was it possible he'd let his mom off the hook simply so he could work with Kim?

Before he could fully consider that bomb, his mom said, "You're as stubborn as I am, and you know it. If you'd really wanted to get rid of Kim, you would have by now. Instead, you're coaching her son's baseball team."

His jaw went slack, then hardened. Of course she knew he'd filled in for the team's regular coach. News traveled fast in Moonlight Cove. He should have expected this parry from his mom. Should have seen it coming from a mile away.

He let out a heavy breath. "I think you're all wrong, Mom." What else could he say? He liked Kim, sure, and he'd enjoyed coaching the team.

But the last thing he needed was for his mom to latch on to trying to get him and Kim together. Good thing she didn't know they'd kissed.

"Maybe I'm wrong, maybe not. But I can see I've hit a nerve," she said, narrowing her eyes a bit. "Wonder why?"

Actually, she *had* hit on something, and her insights didn't sit well with him. But he had to downplay his mother's intuition or she'd be planning his wedding by nightfall. "You're way off base, Mom, really you are. Kim needed a job, that's it. Don't read anything more into the situation. I'm only coaching for a week, and you'll be coming back to work soon."

"And then you're going to cut her loose, without a job?"

Words stuck in his mouth. Could he really do that to Kim? Be that heartless? Keep her from saving enough money for her first term of college?

Trouble was, he wasn't sure that he could.

After Seth and his mom talked, he spent the day in the safety of his office as usual, working on paperwork, letting his mom help the customers. He did his best to put their conversation out of his mind, even though the points she'd made bothered him.

How *was* he going to take Kim's job away from her?

Late in the afternoon, he went to collect receipts. Just as he reached the cash register, the bells over the door rang with an abrupt clang.

Seth looked up and saw his dad bluster into

the store and make a beeline for Seth, his look a glower.

Surprise ricocheted through Seth. Even though his dad used to own The Sports Shack, he didn't come in very often. Mainly because Mom was here all the time. Or had been until she'd mutinied when Kim showed up on the scene.

If only Dad had avoided Mom when they had been married. There wouldn't have been so many skirmishes in the Graham household. Maybe life would have been less chaotic.

Today, Dad was clearly on his way to his favorite fishing hole; he was dressed for angling in cargo pants and a fishing vest, along with a beat-up Mariners cap shoved down over his graying but still full head of hair.

He was a tall man with bad style, and as usual, his pants were too short and his ancient shirt trailed out over his paunch. His complexion was sportsman ruddy from so many hours spent in the sun. Skin cancer waiting to happen if you asked Seth.

Seth chewed on the inside of his lip. Maybe Dad was here because he needed worms or something.

Dad glanced around from underneath low-drawn eyebrows. "Where's your mom?" he drilled out.

"Hey, Dad, nice to see you, too," Seth said drily.

He was used to his dad's brusque attitude. Used to, but not thrilled with.

"Sorry," Dad replied. He yanked on the bill of his hat. "I'm just a bit…upset, that's all."

Before Seth could respond, his mom popped up from aisle one, where she was cleaning the lower level display, although how she could find anything to clean after Kim had put her back into sprucing up the place was beyond him. Between the two women, a guy could eat off the floor.

"I'm right here, Joe." She walked over to the counter, a feather duster in her hand. "What's up?" she asked patiently, putting a hand on one hip.

"What's this I hear about you dating Floyd Simpson?" Dad asked without preamble.

Seth swallowed. *Here come the fireworks.*

Mom glared at Dad, then set the duster on the front counter. "I'm not *dating* him," she said. "I'm just going out to dinner with him."

"Sounds like a date to me," his dad groused. "Really, Marie. Floyd Simpson?"

Mom picked up a pencil from the counter and jammed it behind her ear, then began shoving her way around the register.

Seth slid sideways and back a bit, giving her a clear path.

"What's wrong with Floyd?" She opened a drawer and began rifling through it. "He's a very nice man."

"If you're into fishing." Dad spat the last word as if it were poison.

She looked Dad up and down, her lip curled. "Which you obviously are."

"Yeah." Dad snorted. "But you're not."

"And you complained about that the whole time we were married."

"I thought it would be nice if we had some common interests, that's all."

"Then why didn't you just take up knitting?" she asked acidly. "Oh, that's right, it doesn't involve a rod and reel or a gun, so it's not worth doing. How could I forget?"

Dad's face reddened even more. "I want to know if you're dating Floyd."

"I told you, we're going to dinner and a movie, that's all." She huffed and crossed her arms over her chest. "Not that it's any of your business."

"What are you going to do? Date every single geezer in town?"

"If I want to, yes," Mom retorted, raising her chin so high it looked painful. "We're divorced, remember?"

"Oh, believe me, I haven't forgotten," Dad said, his voice coated in bitterness. "You remind me every chance you get, now, don't you?"

"Yet you managed to forget about your family three days a week?" Mom snorted. "So typical of you."

Mom studied her ex for a second. "Wait a minute." She narrowed her blue eyes. "Are you… jealous?"

Dad froze for a moment, looking stricken. He gave way a step, but remained silent.

Seth looked back and forth between his parents, his stomach pitching.

Clearly Mom had read the situation right, though. His dad *was* jealous. And probably hurt, too. Hurt and in pain and lashing out at things he had no control over.

Seth shuddered. Love. Toxic if you asked him.

"Okay, okay," Seth said. He'd played umpire with his parents before, he'd play the role again. That was the dynamic—his parents fighting, with him caught in the middle. He hated the cycle; it had deeply wounded him as a kid. But he knew better than to hope for any kind of harmony between them, even for his sake. Too many bad feelings tainted the family.

Sad. Heart smashing, actually.

"Hey, you two. This is no place for a squabble," Seth forced out past the tightness in his throat, gesturing around the store. "A customer might come in."

And he needed a break from the perpetual conflict between his parents. Dealing with the results was gut-wrenching. "You two need to take this somewhere else."

Dad shook his head, his mouth pressed into a thin line. "No, no, there's nothing to take anywhere." He looked at Seth's mom, his eyes reflecting what appeared to be a combination of regret, anger and resignation. "As usual, she's said it all."

And with that, he turned and marched out of the store, the bells over the door jangling hollowly in his wake.

Seth watched him go, his heart just as empty.

"Of all the nerve." Mom snatched up the feather duster. With a shake of her head and a *tsking* sound she went back to the aisle where she'd been cleaning before Dad had arrived.

Seth was left alone at the front counter, his stomach twisted into a pretzel the size of the ones they served at Safeco Field.

This is what relationships did to people. He'd be crazy to let Kim hang around. Absolutely crazy.

He'd have to let her go soon.

Chapter Thirteen

It was a beautiful day in Moonlight Cove. A light ocean breeze blew, cooling off the baseball field a bit, bringing the scent of the sea three blocks away to the group gathered at the elementary school field for Dylan's team's first baseball game.

Even with the fresh breeze, the day was warm for the Washington coast, and Kim wished she'd worn shorts or capris instead of jeans for her first stint as assistant coach. She'd shed her sweatshirt long ago.

She looked over at Seth standing near the third/home baseline, noting for the hundredth time that he *had* worn below-the-knee athletic shorts today. He held a clipboard and wore a whistle around his neck. Cute; he was obviously taking his coaching duties very seriously.

The umpire yelled a call that went right by Kim,

and she realized she needed to pay more attention to the game and less attention to Seth.

Yeah, right.

She hadn't been able to ignore him at all this week at work. She kept dwelling on their kiss, their fun time together coaching and their heart-to-heart conversations.

But something with Seth had changed since the first practice. He had resumed his post in his office ever since she'd come back from her day off. That should be a good thing, right? So why did it feel like something was…missing?

She didn't have an answer for that. But she did know that she didn't like his holing up back there by himself; being so solitary wasn't good for a person. But she realized his creating space between them was probably best. Prudent.

She had to stop being so preoccupied with him, so she quit daydreaming and refocused on the game.

It was the bottom of the ninth inning, and the score was tied zero to zero because few of the boys on either team had played baseball before and most were clueless about the game.

Dylan walked to the batter's box and clunked the dirt off his shoes with the bat just as Seth had taught him. How cute was that?

Kim bit her lip, hoping Dylan could at least hit the ball this time around. He'd been hitless the whole game, which didn't bother her as long as he was having fun. But his striking out was bothering him—big time. He really wanted to be "just like Mr. Graham." And to Dylan, that meant sending the ball over the forest along with sending every base runner in to score.

To Dylan, Seth apparently embodied everything that made a great baseball player.

Hero respect, for sure. Again, she prayed that Dylan wouldn't be hurt and disappointed when Seth was, inevitably, no longer in their lives. She'd need to ask for God's help about how to handle that dicey situation for sure. She felt better knowing she had an ally in Him.

Intent on doing her job as the batting manager—aka kiddie baseball wrangler—she turned around and called, "Jordan, you're on deck. Charlie, you're in the hole." Seth's baseball lingo had worn off on her.

She looked up and waved to Aunt Rose, who was sitting in the stands with her daisy trimmed hat at a jaunty angle on her head. Rose waved back, then stood up and cupped her hands around her mouth like a megaphone. "Come on, Dyl," she shouted, sounding more like a trucker than an older lady. "You've got this."

Kim looked back to Dylan, her nerves jumping. He stepped into the box.

"That's it, Dylan," Seth called from his position, clapping. "Choke up on the bat a bit…good job."

Dylan got into his proper batting stance and stared intently at the pitcher. He looked kind of funny wearing the huge black batting helmet—very top-heavy, actually—but his body language screamed intensity and focus.

"Nice work," Seth said. "Just keep your eye on the ball, and everything will fall into place."

Kim held her breath as the pitcher wound up and threw the ball…

…and, *whack,* Dylan connected, hitting a high infield bouncer!

The crowd cheered. Dylan yipped, dropped the bat and ran toward first. The boy on second hightailed it to third.

But the pitcher somehow snagged the ball and gave it a pretty good throw to first. The first baseman, who seemed to be the only kid on either team who had much experience using a glove, caught the pitcher's throw, and stepped on the bag just as Dylan came barreling down the first baseline.

And Dylan was…out.

Kim's heart sank. She fought the urge to hide her eyes, sure he was going to be so disappointed he hadn't gotten on base.

She looked across the field at Dylan, expecting tears. Instead, he was jumping in the air as he ran back toward the dugout. "Did you see, Coach? I hit the ball!"

Grinning, Seth high-fived Dylan when he reached him. "I saw, and it was fantastic! You did your job just like you were supposed to."

Dylan glowed with pride. "Thanks."

Kim's heart pulsed. Seth had been nothing but patient with the team this week, and that was saying a lot given how unfocused the boys were proving to be. On top of that, he had a real knack for coaching in a positive way, for building up their confidence while instilling in them a really good sense for the mechanics of the game.

She liked the way he approached things.

Kim looked around to make sure Jordan was ready to bat. She saw him standing there, his helmet on, his face pressed into a serious expression.

"You okay?" she asked him.

He nodded. "Coach told me that he has lot of faith in me."

"Yes, I'm sure he does," Kim replied, her jaw slack. An idea niggled at her.

Finding faith…

She shook her head, concentrating on the game. "You can do it, Jordan."

Seth had insisted on this particular batting lineup, explaining to her before the game that putting the least confident player in the key third or fourth position would be a good confidence builder for Jordan. Seth had added that he really felt Jordan would come through for the team.

Bless Seth for that.

Jordan headed toward the batter's box.

"Okay, Jordan," Seth said, meeting him partway to the mound. He put a hand on the boy's shoulder. "Remember. NERF ball."

Kim held her breath. The game had come down to this one at bat. It was a lot of pressure for a kid, but she had confidence Seth knew what he was doing.

Jordan stepped into the batter's box, and Seth backed away to his coaching position.

Focused, Jordan wound up and bravely waited for the first throw. He flinched on the first two pitches, drawing two strikes.

Seth clapped. "Come on Jordan, piece of cake. You've seen what this guy has. Go for it!"

Kim gripped the backstop.

Jordan set up, and then the third pitch left the pitcher's hands. Jordan swung…and connected!

It was a wobbly hit off the base of the bat, and it landed in a puff of dirt three feet from Jordan. Like a bunt, but not.

The spectators erupted.

Jordan ran toward first, just as Seth had taught him, and the catcher threw off his mask, hunting for the ball.

"Go, Jordan, go!" Kim screamed, jumping up and down.

She jerked her gaze to Xavier, cruising to home plate. It was going to be close…

The catcher spotted the ball as it rolled toward the pitcher's mound. To his credit, he scrambled into the dirt to retrieve the ball. He popped up and made a great throw to first—but he didn't step on home plate!

Kim quickly shifted her gaze to the batter. Jordan made it to first before the first baseman caught the ball and the ump called Jordan safe— yes!—and Xavier made it home and…scored a run! Jordan had batted in the winning run!

They'd won the game!

Thank You, God.

Chaos spilled from the dugout and the stands. Kim lifted her hands in the air in jubilation, dancing. Seth ran out and met Jordan, patting his narrow back on the way in, and the team cheered together around the dugout.

Kim saw Seth coming toward her, a huge smile on his handsome face, his baseball cap askew. Amid the boys' laughter, with the smell of the baseball field and grass rising around her and the sunshine warming her shoulders, Seth hugged her tight, his strong arms holding her close.

The embrace only lasted a moment, but being

near him was wondrous. Her heart pounded and she fought the need to hold on a bit longer.

He pulled away, his eyes full of merriment. "We won!"

"I know!" she replied, returning his smile, relishing his happiness. "Great job."

He reached out and squeezed her upper arm. "Thanks. I had a great assistant."

Their eyes met and held, and then he yanked his gaze away, backed up and whistled loudly between his teeth.

The boys froze.

"Sharks!" Seth called, waving his arms. "Let's all settle down so we can go line up and shake hands with the other team. Then meet by the bench before you head home," he added.

Obediently, the Sharks ran to the field and lined up, some of them skipping. Kim and Seth followed behind.

The two teams filed by each other, acknowledging a good game, and Kim noticed Seth said some encouraging words to each player on the other team as he gave them high fives.

After handshakes with the other coaches, the whole team met in the dugout.

Seth took off his cap. "First, up, gentlemen, I just want to congratulate you on your first win." A chorus of whoops rose up from the group of boys, and a smile trembled over Kim's lips.

He then proceeded to name each boy, along with mentioning a positive contribution each had made to the team, shaking hands with them one by one, his big hand engulfing theirs with a firm, respectful handshake,

Kim listened and watched, her heart lifting.

Seth went on. "And I also want to tell everyone how proud of you I am. You all played a good game and really worked together as a team." He put his hand on his heart, gazing at the kids. "I've had a great time, and I've learned a lot about myself. Thank you for the privilege of coaching you."

Her eyes burning, Kim drew a shaky breath. She'd learned a lot about him, too. He was a truly excellent man, one with a huge heart. He'd been nothing but a positive role model for these young, impressionable boys.

Her breath caught. He had a lot to give to some lucky gal, and he deserved a woman who could love him fully and completely and give him her heart.

What if she could be that woman?

Grinning from ear to ear, Seth heaved the equipment bag over his shoulder and looked at Dylan, loving the glow on the kid's face. Nothing like winning a baseball game to get a team pumped up. These would be happy memories for everybody.

He felt that winning glow, too, and had loved coaching the boys, a new and very cool experience for him, despite his initial reservations.

"Coach, how about you come to dinner at Auntie Rose's?" Dylan said, jumping up and down. He wore his baseball cap backward, and, as usual, his blond hair stuck out underneath the blue and white hat. "She just left to make fried chicken 'cause it's my favorite, and 'cause we won the game!"

Seth hesitated. The game was over. Kim had said she didn't want Dylan getting attached to him. He had to respect her wishes, even if they rankled a bit. Okay, a lot. More than he'd expected, actually.

"Oh, I don't know." Seth put the equipment bag down and looked to Kim, quirking his eyebrow questioningly. "I'm sure your mom and aunt have other plans." Stock answer. Would Dylan buy it?

Before Kim could respond, Dylan jumped in and said, "No, they don't. Mom told me so when I asked."

No chance. The kid was smart.

Kim flushed and raised a hand. "He's right," she said. "Although, to be fair, I didn't know why he was asking."

Implying if she had known, she would have said no?

"But you don't mind, do you?" Dylan piped in,

his big blue eyes wide. "I really want Coach to see the puppies."

Seth paused, again looking to Kim to make the decision. In his eyes it was just dinner, but in hers…well, he knew the score there. She'd made her wishes clear.

Her face clouded with uneasiness, and she looked as if she were trying to decide on the fly whether to swing or not.

"Please, Mom?" Dylan begged. "I promise I'll go to bed early."

She sighed, looking at the ground, then gave Dylan a grudging nod. "Okay. If it means that much to you."

Surprise shot through Seth. He'd been sure she'd say no. What did it mean that she hadn't?

Nothing. Absolutely nothing. She was just giving in for her son's sake. This was all about Dylan. As it should be.

"But no complaining when it's time to turn in, all right?" she said firmly, sounding like the caring mother she obviously was. The one that impressed Seth so much.

"All right!" Dylan crowed, clapping. "Wait till you see the puppies, Coach. They're so cool. Especially Cleo." He ran toward the parking lot. "Come on. Let's go."

Seth held back and looked at Kim, trying to read her. "Are you sure about this?" he asked, willing to do whatever she wanted, even if that meant going home alone as usual. She called the shots on her son. "I'll back out if you want me to."

"And disappoint Dylan? No." She smiled brightly, but he was pretty sure he saw a glint of worry in her eyes. "Looks like you're coming over." She gestured toward the parking lot with a stiff hand. "Let's go pig out on fried chicken and play with puppies."

"All right," Seth said, picking up the equipment bag.

They headed toward the cars, silent. Seth looked across the short expanse of parking lot and saw Dylan standing at Kim's compact car, his freckled cheeks pressed into a joyful smile.

As Seth and Kim drew near, Dylan said, "I'm so happy you're coming over, Coach. This is going to be fun!"

Seth couldn't help but return the kid's grin. "I know you're right. Hanging out with you will be a great way to end a great day."

"No kidding," Dylan said. "We won the game, and you're coming over. This is the best day I've had since we moved here."

Seth's heart pulled tight, but he tried to ignore the feeling and, instead, focused on living up to his title of Coach. "Yeah. Playing baseball is really fun whether you win or lose, though. Right?" He held up a hand to high-five Dylan, looking briefly at Kim.

She nodded approvingly, as if to thank Seth for taking his coaching duties so seriously.

He realized that her good opinion meant a lot to him. New concept for sure.

"Right!" Dylan replied, jumping up and slapping Seth's hand.

A sense of accomplishment filtered through Seth. Who would have guessed he'd enjoy being a positive influence on kids so much?

As he loaded the equipment into his rig with Dylan by his side, excitedly chatting him up about everything from the details of the game to what they were having for dessert, Seth realized just how attached to him Dylan was becoming.

Attached. As in *connected*.

On cue, engrained, familiar doubts sunk their hooks into Seth. Was he making a mistake?

He looked down at Dylan's shining face. No. No way was making Dylan happy a mistake. He couldn't disappoint the kid. He wasn't heartless. Besides, he liked Dylan.

He'd just have to work on not liking the kid's pretty, appealing mom quite so much.

Chapter Fourteen

Kim drove Dylan home from the game, her palms damp. She'd given in to him again and had agreed to have Seth over for dinner.

Why couldn't she say no to her son, aside from the fact that he was cute as all get-out, and was very good at getting what he wanted?

Before she could search too far within herself to dig out the answer, Dylan looked at her, his head tilted to the side. "Mom, why don't you like Coach?"

She swallowed. Trust a seven-year-old to ask the really tough questions. "I…I don't dislike Mr. Graham, honey." This situation would be easier if she *did* dislike Seth. Or was completely indifferent to him. Way easier. The fact was, she was so far from being indifferent, it wasn't even funny. It was scary.

"Then why do you keep trying to stop him from doing stuff with us?"

Surprise had her jaw loose. Guess her son was more perceptive than she'd thought. And even though she might *possibly* be falling for Seth—there, she'd admitted it—she didn't know how he felt about her. She still had to protect Dylan in case Seth bolted.

Or she could have faith in Seth.

She took a deep breath and slowly exhaled, then gripped the steering wheel so tightly her knuckles turned white. She looked at Dylan, words stuck in her throat.

"What's wrong, Mom?" Dylan wrinkled his nose. "Don't you trust him?"

Kim almost drove off the road.

Out of the mouths of babes…

Unable to formulate a response, Kim made a big show of adjusting the rearview mirror, catching her own panicked gaze as she did so. Okay. So she was on her own here. Just the way she wanted things. So be it.

She cleared her throat. "Um…of course I do, sweetie."

"Then I don't see what you're so worried about. We trust Coach. We like him. That's all that matters, right?"

As Kim pulled into Rose's driveway, she opened her mouth to respond, but no words would come out. She simply sat there, gaping like a dying fish, stunned silent by the wisdom in her son's observations.

As soon as the car stopped, Dylan jumped out. "I'm going to go see if Benny will bring over the puppies later."

"Okay," Kim replied, watching him run through a well-worn break in the hedge between Rose and Benny's yards.

Kim turned off the car and slumped in her seat, as pieces of conversations she'd had with Seth flashed through her brain, along with several key words. Words she'd used when talking to Seth.

Faith. Trust. Believe.

She'd told Seth that faith begat faith, and that he had to have enough faith in God to trust He would answer Seth's prayers. Faith was faith was faith. With one, you had the other. And she took those words to heart, trusted in how they defined her relationship with God.

But she wasn't, she realized breathlessly, applying that belief in faith to her relationship with Seth.

How could she ask Seth to have faith and trust in God when she didn't have the same in the man who had been nothing but wonderful to her and her son?

She'd seen what kind of man he was. Kind, gentle, caring. And loving.

She had faith in him. She saw that now. She had for quite a while, or she would never have let him spend so much time with Dylan.

Feeling as if her world had rotated on its axis, Kim let out a shaky breath and got out of her car. So she had faith in Seth. What did that mean for her future?

At the moment the answer to that question was too overwhelming to contemplate.

Seth sat next to Kim on Rose's front porch. His stomach was full of the best fried chicken, potato salad and corn bread he'd ever eaten. Rose had promised strawberry shortcake later, the much-anticipated dessert Dylan had been chattering about by the car.

Rose, of course, had been the epitome of hospitality, even though Seth had gleaned from the surprised look on her face when they'd arrived for dinner that she'd had her fears about him and Kim spending time together.

He grunted inwardly. He knew his reputation as a ladies' man around town, even if he didn't think it was deserved.

Benny had joined them for dinner, and he and Rose were inside watching reruns of Rose's favorite show, *Designing Women*. Seth figured Benny must have it bad for Rose if he was willing to sit through reruns for her.

Kim sat next to him, looking impossibly lovely in the waning light of dusk. The sun, hanging low in the sky, streaked her hair with gold, and her gorgeous eyes glowed a dark, vibrant topaz. She'd put on a pale pink sweater that hinted at the delicate color in her cheeks.

Dylan and his favorite puppy, Cleo, were running around the grassy front yard, playing. His laughs and the dog's joyful barks carried on the breeze, bringing an unusual sense of satisfaction and calm over Seth; in the technology age, it was good to see a young kid so carefree, so content just to roughhouse with an energetic puppy.

"He loves that puppy, doesn't he?" Seth asked Kim.

"Adores her." Kim leaned her arms on her knees. "I wish I could buy the pup for him, but I don't think that's in the cards."

He leaned back onto his elbows and stretched his legs out. "Why not?"

"It's not practical for us to have a dog until we have our own place."

"Ah, I see." Not surprising she'd want a place of her own. She wanted to make it by herself. He understood that. And admired her desire to be independent.

He looked at Dylan and the puppy rolling around on the grass together. "It's going to be hard for him to see her go."

"Well, Benny has decided to keep her, so Dyl can come visit. But it won't be the same as having his own dog."

"No, it won't."

Kim looked at Seth, her eyes questioning. "Did you ever have a dog growing up?"

"Nope. My mom and dad could never agree on what kind to get. Mom wanted a lap dog, and Dad wanted a hunting dog." Seth shrugged, attempting to hide the hurt jabbing its way through him. "They never could find a way to compromise." Not even for their kids.

The breeze kicked up, blowing Kim's hair around her face. "Yeah, you told me on our picnic that your parents fought a lot."

He hesitated, reluctant, as always, to talk about his dysfunctional family. But he'd already opened this subject a few days ago. Would it really hurt to stick another toe through the door? He hoped not.

"All the time," he replied, barely moving his lips. "They still don't get along."

She put her hand on his arm briefly. "That must be really hard."

The spot where she'd touched him glowed with warmth. He snorted his agreement. "Drives me crazy, actually."

"Sounds like you need someone to talk to."

"Maybe." He shifted uneasily, looking out over

the yard at nothing, really. "But to tell the truth, I've never been comfortable talking about my family."

"Because?" she asked softly, her eyes moving over his face.

He looked down. "Too ashamed, I guess." He'd never told anyone that. Why was he opening up now? With her? What was it about her that pulled that kind of personal stuff out of him?

"Well, you know, you could always talk to God about this. He's a good listener, and He doesn't judge."

"Is that what you would do?" he questioned before he could call the words back. In for a penny.

"I would," she replied. "Plus, I'd probably find someone else to confide in, talk things out with. It's always good to interact with people, you know?"

Even though he didn't really agree with her way of thinking, he respected her input enough to admit, "Opening up to others…well, it's never been easy for me."

"Uh-huh. I see that in you."

He tugged his eyebrows together. "Really?"

"You bet. It's kind of like you put up a wall."

"Not consciously," he said, feeling his face flush.

She tilted her head in assent. "I'm sure you don't

even really think about your wall," she said graciously. "But it's still there."

He'd never given his habit of subconsciously putting up barriers much thought. Interesting. But he wasn't sure her observation was cause for much consideration. He'd never been particularly introspective.

She chimed in before he could get his thoughts together and respond. "Maybe you just haven't found the right person to talk to." She regarded him, looking deep into his eyes. "Sometimes that can make all the difference."

"I doubt it," he said, straight up, returning her gaze. "I've never put much stock in talking to another person about personal stuff." Not even Drew. That just didn't work for Seth. Or come easy.

"Well, you should. With two trustworthy confidantes, you can't lose."

"Win-win. Is that what you're saying?"

"Pretty much," she said, nodding.

He wasn't sure he agreed with her. Maybe confiding in others and God on a regular basis was doable...but probably not. It wasn't his style.

She sat silent for a long moment, her eyes turned toward the front yard. She cleared her throat. "Listen," she eventually said, watching Dylan and the puppy romp together. "The church singles group is meeting next week for a progressive dinner. Are you going?"

He stayed quiet for a pensive moment. Drew had mentioned the activity the other day and had also asked Seth if he wanted to attend. Seth had said he'd go, mainly because he hadn't seen Drew in a while and wanted to spend some time with his best friend.

But another evening spent with Kim? Without the buffer of Dylan around? That was a different animal.

But there would be lots of other people at the dinner. Loads. It wasn't as if he and the woman sitting beside him would be alone together.

Unfortunately...

He shoved that thought into mental oblivion as best he could.

"You want to think about it for a while?" she asked softly. "No pressure."

"Sure," he said, trying to sound casual, noncommittal in his usual way. "Can I let you know?"

"Anytime. As long as you can whip up an entrée for twelve on a moment's notice."

He pulled in his chin and stared at her wordlessly.

"Kidding," she said, flipping a hand in the air. "Lighten up, will ya? You won't have to cook."

He laughed under his breath. "Be thankful for

that. My cooking abilities don't go much beyond grilled cheese and canned tomato soup."

Just then, Dylan called out. "Hey, Coach. Come play with me and Cleo."

"The general has spoken." Seth squeezed Kim's hand, then let go and stood. "Demanding, isn't he?"

"Very," she said, quirking one corner of her mouth up. "Thank you for spending time with him. It means a lot to him, you know."

"Glad to do it," he replied frankly. "He's a great kid."

"Well, if it's any comfort, you don't seem to have trouble relating to him."

She was right; interacting with Dylan came much easier. "I've thought about that, and I think it's because kids are less likely to inflict a wound in my mind."

"Maybe because you sense their innate innocence?"

"Exactly."

"That's my take, too," she said, smoothing her glossy hair behind one ear. "Sometimes, as I said, I can sense you…holding back. But you don't hold back with Dylan and the boys."

"Thank you for showing me that," he said. "You've managed to help me see something I never have." Maybe he could apply being more comfortable with kids to his other relationships, now that Kim had shown him the connection.

Dylan called out again. "Coach, come on."

"Gotta go play," Seth said. "I'll think about this conversation for a long time to come."

He went down the steps and jogged to the spot in the yard where Dylan sat with Cleo on his lap.

Just as Seth reached him, Dylan sprang up and ran away from Seth. "Bet you can't catch me!" Dylan shouted.

Cleo followed in his wake, yipping.

"Oh-ho!" Seth replied, giving chase, a freeing sense of spontaneity taking over. "I bet I can!"

They ran around the yard, man, boy and dog, as the sun made its way toward the horizon. The breeze blew the smell of the ocean across Seth's face, filling him with a sense of exhilaration and freedom.

Seth let Dylan stay just out of his reach for a while, making a game out of the chase, and Dylan skipped around, giggling. Cleo joined the fray, staying right on Dylan's heels.

But eventually, Seth turned on the afterburners, grabbed Dylan from behind and hauled him into the air. "I've got you now!"

Dylan squealed, his eyes shining, a happy smile on his face. Cleo barked, then got into the doggy play stance with her rear in the air and barked again.

Instead of putting Dylan down, it seemed the most natural thing in the world to hug the boy. He smelled of fresh air and fried chicken and laundry detergent. Dylan threw his arms around Seth and hugged him back.

Seth's chest tightened, ice seeming to melt away from somewhere inside him, and he looked over Dylan's shoulder to where Kim still sat on the front porch. She looked on, smiling lovingly, completing the picture perfectly.

A profound thought hit him. Wow. Was this what being part of a *functional* family was like?

Stunned, Seth moved his gaze to Cleo. She stared up at him and Dylan, looked as if she clearly approved, then plopped down, her tail wagging, clearly worn out. But happy as all get out.

At that moment, Seth knew how the ball of fluff felt. The whole family-with-Kim-and-Dylan scenario kind of appealed to him.

As did Kim's deep and abiding faith.

A rogue thought crashed into him. Was it at all possible letting down his guard—his walls, as Kim had said—might be a good thing?

Chapter Fifteen

"So what's up with you and Seth?" Lily asked, balancing an apple pie in one hand and a chocolate cake in the other. She set them both on the dining room table.

They were on the dessert leg of the singles group progressive dinner, at Lily's house. Molly Kent, who owned the pet store on Main Street, Bow Wow Boutique, and Phoebe, the owner of I Scream for Ice Cream, whom Kim had already met, were also in the spacious dining room, helping put out refreshments.

"I'm not sure," Kim said, taking the plastic off the plate of chocolate chip cookies she'd brought.

Lily frowned. "What do you mean, you're not sure?" She grabbed a cake server from the buffet. "Do you like him?"

Kim folded the plastic in her hands. "I guess," she said, downplaying, even to herself.

"So what's the problem?" Phoebe asked, her brow line arched. "He certainly appears to like you."

"Why do you say that?" Kim tried to ignore the unexpected dart of pleasure that streaked through her at Phoebe's observation.

"He hasn't taken his eyes off you the whole night, that's why," Molly—a cute, petite redhead—said, her green eyes glinting.

Kim's face warmed, and her heart skipped a beat. "Really?"

"Really. Trust us, he likes you. I've never seen him this smitten," Lily said, returning to the kitchen, leaving Kim in the dining room with Molly and Phoebe.

Smitten.

Kim pressed a hand to her chest and closed her eyes briefly, searching for good sense, reminding herself that nothing had changed.

Or had it? She'd been working for Seth for three weeks now, and had seen what a good man he truly was.

And Dylan adored him…

"What's wrong?" Molly asked, leaning in, her green eyes blinking. "You could do way worse than Seth."

"Oh, I know," Kim said, nodding. "But…little by little, no matter what I do, the more I like him, and I shouldn't, the more scared I get. You should have seen him with Dylan and the puppy from next door. Seth was amazing." She was rambling now, but she kept going, unable to hold back the floodgates. "I'd always planned to move to Seattle, be totally on my own, you know, so no one could let me down."

Phoebe nodded.

"But Dylan, well, he trusts Seth, and…I've discovered I do, too. Lately I've been wondering if it would be okay to allow myself to give in to my feelings for Seth." She wrung her hands. "I want to stay true to my goals, but I can't help but think that I'm not seeing the forest for the trees." Very confusing, indeed.

"Maybe you need to realize that not doing everything on your own is all right," Phoebe said, setting out the cups. "Of course, there's a trade-off—isn't there always? But maybe sacrificing some of your independence is worth it for a guy like Seth." She smiled. "Hey, he likes your kid, right? Not all guys are so good with children."

"You're right," Kim said, her head spinning. "I'm just so…confused. The more time I spend with Seth…and my son's gushing about 'Coach' while he was getting ready for bed last night… well, that socked me right in the heart."

"Yeah, I bet," Phoebe said, smoothing her

untamed head of blond curls back with one hand. "You should think twice before letting him go, though."

Lily came back into the room carrying a pitcher of lemonade.

"Trouble is, I'm pretty sure he doesn't want a romantic relationship," Kim replied. "He seems dead set against any kind of emotional commitment, and from what I hear, he's dated around quite a bit."

Molly frowned. "Really? Where'd you hear that?"

"From my aunt," Kim said. "She called him a playboy."

"Hmm," Molly said, narrowing her gaze. "I guess he's dated some, but not really *that* much. True, he's played the field, but he's not what I would consider a playboy." She looked at Phoebe, her gaze questioning. "Would you?"

"Definitely not," Phoebe said, leaning a hip against the table.

Molly looked at Lily. "How about you?"

"Nope, not really," Lily replied, putting the lemonade down. "Actually, I think the playboy thing might be driven by a generational attitude. Someone dates more than two people in a few years, and suddenly the older tongues are wagging."

"So you think my aunt overstated the situation?"

Kim asked, a strange hope starting to glow in her heart. Was it possible she'd been given exaggerated information?

"Definitely," Lily, Phoebe and Molly all said together, nodding their brunette, blond and auburn heads in perfect time.

Kim shook her head. "I don't know. He has a lot of baggage of his own, and he's admitted he has difficulty letting people close."

"Oh, sure," Phoebe said. "Seth keeps to himself a lot, especially around strangers. But deep inside, he's a softy, and he's a loyal friend to those of us who've known him since we were kids. When the right woman comes along, he'll fall like a ton of bricks." She gave Kim a significant look, implying she thought Kim might be the "right woman."

Kim gnawed on a lip. "I'm not so sure."

"Trust us. We wouldn't steer you wrong," Lily said, obviously speaking for all of them.

Kim was left reeling. Admitting she had feelings for Seth would be a huge leap for her. And she was trying *not* to leap these days. She was trying to be cautious. How else was she going to learn to stand alone when she moved to Seattle?

But, oh, the thought of being with Seth, letting herself lean on him. Having him in her life sounded amazing.

Lily stepped back, looking over the massive display on the table. "I think we're ready." With a satisfied smile she went over to the arched entrance leading from the dining room to the living room. "Come on, everybody," she called. "Dessert's on."

The other attendees trickled in to chow down, Seth and Drew bringing up the rear.

As usual, Kim's breathing hitched when she saw Seth.

He wore stylish jeans and a white button-down shirt, untucked. He'd gotten some sun during baseball practices, and his skin had darkened just enough that his blue eyes stood out in a very attractive way.

He and Drew were talking, and Seth laughed at something Drew said. His straight teeth flashed, glowing like pearls against his tanned skin. He glanced over midsmile and winked at Kim.

Her tummy fluttered.

Then he said something to Drew, clapped his friend on the back and headed her way. She smiled, trying to look normal, her mouth quivering as one wild thought tumbled through her mind.

Would it be rash to throw caution to the ground and admit she was falling for Seth?

He stepped near and touched the small of her back. Heat and tingles spread through her, and she almost fell into a heap of conflict right there in the middle of the dining room.

"What can I get you?" he said, gesturing to the table full of scrumptious-looking desserts.

I'll take a little sanity with my pie, thank you very much.

Seth drove Kim home in his rig after the progressive dinner. It had been a fantastic evening; he'd never enjoyed time spent with friends more.

Friends…

As the night had gone on, he had sensed something changing inside him…something he couldn't quite put his finger on. It was as if his whole being was lighter. Happier, and more at ease. And certainly less closed off. Less wary of forming some tentative connections.

As he navigated the short distance to Rose's house, he did allow himself to think about how at peace Kim had looked when the group had prayed before going their separate ways at the end of the evening. She'd had her eyes shut, and he could sense that she was internalizing the prayer, using the entreaty to foster her strong bond with God.

Was that path toward having new faith one he wanted to follow? Or *could* follow? "So," he said, filling in the silence. "You looked pretty serene during the prayer."

"I was. Somehow it always makes me feel good to talk to God."

"What do you say?" he asked. It had been a

long time since he'd really talked to or depended on God.

She gave him a funny look.

"I know, weird question." He took one hand off the steering wheel and rubbed his jaw. "Humor me. That is, if it's not too private."

"Okay." She was silent for a moment. "First, I thank Him for everything He's given me. Then I usually ask for guidance on any particular challenges I'm having in my life." She laughed under her breath. "When Scott left, I had to talk to God about helping me on an hourly basis."

"So He really helped you through the divorce?"

"Definitely. I wouldn't have been able to navigate that emotional minefield on my own. I'm sure of it."

"I like the *sound* of knowing I'll always have a guiding hand in God. But in reality, finding the faith to go there…as I've said before, I'm not sure the faith I need to find more faith is there."

She swiveled toward him. "But you have faith in the boys on the team, right?"

He pulled in his chin. "Yeah. So?"

"So, why do you have faith in a bunch of seven-year-olds, but not in God?"

Her words brought him up short. "That's different."

"No, it isn't," she insisted, her voice intent. "Faith is faith is faith."

"Meaning?" he asked, not sure he was going to like her answer because it might be more intuitive than he was comfortable with. But wasn't she always pushing him to think outside the box?

"Meaning that you have the faith you need to move forward, building a deeper relationship with and trusting in God. You just have to believe God will listen, just as you believe the kids will do their best at baseball."

He was speechless, but his mind was spinning. She'd brought up a really good point about the faith he had in the Sharks. Could he apply that kind of trust in God? Or a woman?

Maybe.

"Have you ever thought that maybe you're afraid to connect with God for the same reason you're afraid to connect to other people?" She gazed directly at him, the dim glow from the passing street lights illuminating her face. "Maybe you feel threatened by letting Him close."

He clenched his hands on the steering wheel and tightened his jaw. Even though she'd hit on a painful truth he didn't like examining, he respected her opinion. "You might be right," he said, inclining his head to the side in tentative agreement. "I've always associated close personal relationships with paying a price, God included."

"Well, there's your problem," she said. "God never extracts a price. He only bestows His wisdom."

"Makes perfect sense when you put it that way," he said truthfully. She'd taught him a lot lately.

He made a left onto Rose's street, feeling as if Kim had peeled away a tightly wound bandage since they'd left Lily's. Did he really want to see what was underneath the protective covering? And was the wound under the bandage even healable? He'd never thought so before.

But now…he had hope. He was able to relate to and have faith in the Sharks. Maybe he could follow suit in other areas in his life.

With Kim. And God.

He cleared his throat. "I really appreciate your insights," he said, leaving it at that. Old, safe habits died hard. He still had his walls. But Kim was breaking them down, one brick at a time. And he wasn't sure he wanted her to stop.

"I'm glad I could help," she said. "It's the least I could do for the guy who saved my life."

Was that all he was to her? Her rescuer? If so, could he deal with just being the guy on the beach who'd saved her life?

No, he realized. Not really. Wow. "We're even now, right?"

"We'll never be even," she replied in a soft voice.

"Nothing I do will ever compare to the risk you took to save me."

Basking in her praise, Seth concentrated on driving for a moment. "So," he said, turning the conversation away from himself. "What challenges are you discussing with God right now?"

She let out an audible breath. "How I'm going to afford college, get my teaching certificate and become completely independent."

"And what have you and God decided?" he asked as he pulled into Rose's driveway, an idea beginning to simmer in the back of his mind. Baseball had been very good to him financially....

"That if I want my dreams to come true, I need to be patient, diligent and trust that He will provide whatever I need."

Seth looked over at her, then put the truck in park and turned off the engine. "And you believe He will provide?" Perhaps through Seth? Intriguing, the thought of helping her dream come true.

"Of course. He's never let me down in the past."

"I have to say, I find your faith in God very admirable, but not something I ever thought I would find." The two ends of the spectrum hadn't ever balanced each other out in his mind in the past.

Maybe that was changing, though.

"Well, for what it's worth, I think you have the

faith you need, right here," she said, a light touch to his chest.

A tingly spot throbbed beneath her hand. "So you believe in me?" No one had ever told him that.

"I believe in you," she said, nodding. "God believes in you, too. But until you believe in yourself, nothing will ever change."

He shifted in the truck seat. "What if I'm happy with my life the way it is?"

She pulled her hand away. "Are you? Happy?"

He stared at the dashboard, words stuck in his throat. A month ago, he would have said yes to being happy in a nanosecond. But now...why was an answer so hard to come up with?

Uncomfortable with the questions and their implications bouncing around in his brain, he went with, "I'm...not sure." Safe, but honest. It was the best he could do.

Kim didn't say anything for a second while Seth's statement sank in. It sounded like he doubted his own happiness. "Is something missing in your life?" she asked, turning toward him. Loaded question, yes. But the answer was somehow important.

He sat silently. "I never really thought so...but, maybe, yes."

That had to be huge for a guy like him to admit. "What do you think it is?" Okay, so she was fishing. But didn't a girl need to know where she stood?

He turned and hit her with those eyes of his, which seemed to glow in the light of the moon like blue fire. "You tell me."

He was being cagey. She got that; it was hard to look inward, especially, she knew, for Seth. He didn't trust in personal relationships. But this discussion was too important for her to let him slide by. She had to be honest and open, given what she'd discovered about her feelings for Seth at the progressive dinner.

Didn't she owe herself that?

She took a deep breath, hanging out on a limb, and said, "Love?"

He stilled. "I never thought I would find love."

Not an outright denial. Okay. She cast the line out again. "Do you think you could find it now?"

He reached out and stroked her cheek, catching her gaze with his. "Maybe."

His touch was soft and compelling, and his words sent hope soaring inside of her. She nuzzled his hand, and with gentle pressure he turned her face toward him. And then he leaned in and kissed her, his breath flowing over her like warm silk.

She kissed him back, feeling as if her heart had grown wings. Warmth and contentment and a feeling of belonging settled over her.

How could she fight her attraction to this man?

He broke the kiss and put his arms around her, pulling her close and murmuring something under his breath. She nestled against his chest, loving being so near him.

Seth's hands stroked her hair, and she'd never felt so protected. So cherished. How could this be wrong?

They sat silently together for a long while, the darkness of the coastal night enveloping them in a cocoon that made her feel as if they were the only two people left in the world.

Maybe things would be easier if they were.

But then he slowly pulled away. "What are we doing?" he asked, his deep voice as compelling as the force of the Pacific Ocean pounding the shore on the other side of Rose's house.

She shook her head and laughed softly, ruefully. "I don't know. It's scary, isn't it?"

He rested his chin on the top of her head, nodding, his arms pulling her even closer. "Sure is." His voice was husky in the darkness. "But I'm feeling braver these days."

His words made her heart soar in a way she'd never felt before. Was it possible he might be able to open his heart to her? "So am I." Amazingly so.

She felt his mouth curve into a smile against her head, and then he moved his mouth down, his rough jaw rasping briefly against her cheek. He whispered in her ear, "I'm glad."

For the first time in forever, her doubts and fears about love faded into the background.

And in that moment of time, as she sat there in Seth's arms feeling safe and on the verge of being loved, she had a tantalizing measure of hope for a future with the wonderful man holding her close.

Chapter Sixteen

Kim got up early Monday morning after dreaming of Seth, her and Dylan being a happy family.

Smiling at the attractive picture the dream painted, she showered, dressed and headed to the kitchen for breakfast, trying to stay on an even keel. Dylan and Rose were still sleeping, so the house was quiet.

Kim made her favorite breakfast of fruit with granola and yogurt and sat eating at Rose's little kitchen table, thinking about Seth.

Inevitably, thoughts of him brought snippets of the dream flashing into her brain; Dylan and Seth had been flying a kite on the beach, with the brilliant sun shining overhead. She'd stood, looking on, happier than she could ever remember being. Dylan had been gazing up at Seth with love shining from his eyes, and Seth had returned the look unabashedly. And then he'd turned his sky-blue gaze to her, and he'd looked at her as if he loved her with all his heart.

Happy family. Mom, Dad and child. A truly wonderful picture, one that was growing more and more compelling with each day that passed. Especially after their kiss and its profound aftermath last night in Seth's truck.

She said a quick prayer, asking for guidance, then settled in to eat. Halfway through breakfast, Rose appeared in her yellow terry robe. She had shadows beneath her eyes and lacked her usual spring in her step.

Concern bubbled through Kim. "What's wrong?"

"Oh, I slept poorly," Rose said, pulling the robe's belt tighter. "I ended up reading in bed most of the night."

Kim stood. Rose was usually a good sleeper and didn't typically fail to get in her eight hours. "Why? What's going on?"

Rose shrugged her slim shoulders. "I guess I'm a bit...distracted."

"About what?" Kim asked, moving over to the stove. She put a teakettle on to boil. A warm cup of tea always seemed to make Rose feel better.

Rose sank into the chair next to the one Kim had been occupying. "Benny asked me out on a date."

Kim grinned. "That's wonderful!"

"I'm not so sure." Rose sighed, then stood up and walked over to the teakettle and stared at it. "I've never really done a lot of dating. It's too… messy."

True. "Maybe you should, especially with Benny." Kim propped a hip against the counter. "You two get along really well, and he's a very nice man."

"That's right, I guess," Rose replied, rubbing at a spot on the tile counter. "But still…I'm nervous about any kind of romance."

"Look at it this way," Kim said. "You guys already spend a lot of time together here. I think it makes sense to go out and do some fun stuff as a couple." Kim arched a brow. "I'm surprised he hasn't asked you out sooner. He obviously has a big crush on you."

Rose's cheeks pinkened, and she waved a hand in the air. "Oh, come now. I wouldn't exactly call it a crush…"

"I would," Kim said, getting the daisy-festooned mugs out of the cupboard. "He can barely speak coherently when you're around."

"Really?" Rose made a big show of pulling the tea bags from the stoneware canister in the corner. "Hmm. I hadn't noticed."

Yeah, sure. "It's true. He really likes you. And he sits through all those reruns of *Designing*

Women," Kim said, arching a brow. "If that isn't devotion, I don't know what is."

Rose plopped the bags into the cups, shaking her head. "If you're right…then I'm scared to death. What if Benny and I don't work out?"

The teakettle started to wail.

"I know what you're talking about, believe me." She had the same worries about her and Seth. Kim turned off the heat and poured the hot water over the fragrant tea bags. "But don't you think you should live your life as fully as possible and see where that living leads?" She took the cups and set them on the table.

After a long pause, Rose moved to the table and sat down. "Maybe." She stirred sugar into her tea, staring at the swirling liquid. "Maybe not."

"I don't like the thought of you alone for the rest of your life, Aunt Rose." She took her aunt's hand in hers. "You deserve someone special."

Rose squeezed Kim's hand. "Do you really believe that?"

"I do," Kim said, sitting down. "Wholeheartedly."

Rose kept stirring her tea, then turned her inquisitive gaze to Kim. "Then why are you trying so hard to deny yourself those same things?"

A chill ran through Kim. "I *have* been doing that, haven't I?"

Rose nodded sagely. "Yes, dear, you have. You're

so intent on protecting your heart because of the past, you can't get over your fear long enough to grab what will make you happy for your future."

Kim let those words sink in, then felt the need to confide in Aunt Rose. "Actually, my fear does fade now and then." Kim blushed. "Seth and I kissed for the second time last night." And they'd sat for a long time, just holding each other close.

Rose took a sip of tea, then looked over the rim of her cup and said, "I know."

"You do? How?"

"I can see the driveway from the living room," Rose said, a knowing expression on her face.

Kim stared at her teacup, her cheeks warming even more. "Oh. Yes. I guess you can."

"Don't be embarrassed," Rose told her, waving a hand in the air. "I was young and in love once myself."

Kim's head shot up. "I'm not in love with Seth."

Or am I?

Admitting her feelings scared her.

"Well, in my opinion you're close, and so is he," Rose said.

The thought of Seth loving Kim made her heart jump in jubilation.

Rose continued. "I think you should grab the man before it's too late."

Kim's mouth dipped. "Two weeks ago you were warning me off Seth. What gives?"

Rose set down her tea. "I've seen Seth up close and personal in the last few days, here at dinner and at Dylan's game. He's shown himself to be a stand-up man and Dylan adores him." She shrugged. "What can I say? He's nice to my grand-nephew and he's nice to you and he saved your life. Guess I've changed my mind."

Kim swallowed. "Honestly?" Trust Rose to see through the pesky weeds to the flower of the matter.

"Honestly," Rose replied. "I see the way you look at Seth."

Kim's face heated. "Is it that obvious?" Why hide the truth?

"A woman in love is always obvious," Rose said.

Before Kim could reply, Dylan walked into the kitchen.

Kim stared. He already had on his baseball practice clothes—including his cap—and his glove hung from his left hand.

"Hey, Dyl," she said, hiding her surprise at his attire. Had he slept in his baseball gear? It was only seven-thirty. "Good morning, sunshine."

"Morning," he said, stopping in the middle of the kitchen. He rubbed his eyes with his ungloved hand. "Morning, Auntie Rose."

"Good morning, dear," Rose said, rising. "Would you like pancakes for breakfast?"

"Yes, please," Dylan replied sleepily.

Rose started getting out the fixings for Dylan's second favorite breakfast.

Kim held out her arms. "Come here, you," she said.

Dylan came over and snuggled up close. He smelled like sleepy kid, all warm and cozy.

She swallowed. "So," she said, pulling his cap off because the bill was poking her in the face. "Why are you already wearing your baseball clothes?"

"Coach said we could play catch today."

Leaning back, she gazed at Dylan and said, "He did? When?"

"When Auntie Rose and I saw him in town yesterday."

Kim chewed on her lip. "Ah, I see." And she did see. Too well. Looked as if it was time to figure out what she was going to do about her feelings for Seth.

While Rose helped Dylan wash his hands at the kitchen sink, Kim mulled over the conversation she and Dylan had had in the car after the baseball game. She reminded herself that she should practice what she preached—she needed to have faith to find faith.

In Seth.

Plus, Aunt Rose was right. Kim needed to take her own advice and put aside her fear and stop letting the past control her future. Easier said than done, yes. But she was willing to make the leap for the reward.

Nothing worth having was easy to come by, right?

She closed her eyes for a moment, letting the truth free within her heart. A warm tide spread through her, wiping all her doubts away. Breathlessly she realized she loved Seth. With everything in her. To echo Dylan's words, that was all that mattered.

Rose and Dylan sat at the table, and Dylan wolfed down three pancakes and two glasses of orange juice, going on and on about baseball practice and Coach.

Kim smiled and held her new feelings close. Now more than ever she was certain she was doing the right thing.

As soon as Dylan was finished eating, Kim rose and picked up his plate and juice glass. "Why don't you go get changed for Vacation Bible School, okay?"

"Okay, Mom," he said, casting her a hopeful look. "Are you gonna let me and Coach play catch later today?"

Kim nodded, her mouth curved into a gentle

smile. "Sure, sweetie. I think that sounds like fun."

"Woo-hoo!" Dylan crowed, pumping a fist in the air. "I can hardly wait!"

Kim couldn't remember when she'd been so happy to say yes to her son. But this wasn't all about pleasing him, oh, no. Letting Seth into their lives was the right thing to do for her, too, the one thing that would make her happy.

A sense of calm spread over her.

When Dylan had left the room, Rose folded her hands on the table and said, "So. You're letting Dylan play catch with Seth. Does this mean you've figured out your feelings for him?"

Kim stood, teacup in hand. "You were right about what you said earlier." She took a deep breath. "I do love Seth." A chill of excitement tinged with apprehension ran through her. Big words, big feelings.

A huge leap for her.

"I thought so." Rose nodded sagely, her eyes sparkling. "So what are you going to do about that?"

Kim started to load the breakfast dishes into the dishwasher, her hands quivering as her calm disappeared, hoping she didn't drop anything. Before long, if she didn't get a handle on her erratic emotions, she'd have to replace every dish in Rose's kitchen. "Well…I guess I have to tell him the truth." The idea of laying her heart bare sent terror shooting through her. Absolute terror.

Rose's brow furrowed. "He has relationship issues, though. How do you think he'll react?"

"I have no idea," Kim said, realizing again that she was going to have to put a lot on the line to tell Seth how she felt. Anxiety gnawed away at her confidence.

"Nothing ventured, nothing gained?" Rose said.

"Exactly. I have to have faith."

A tad breathless, Kim finished the last of the dishes and closed the dishwasher. "Along those lines, are you going to go out on an actual date with Benny?"

"If you can tell Seth that you love him, I can say yes to Benny. I'll go over there after I drop Dylan off at Vacation Bible School, which is at the beach today."

"Great," Kim said, excitement jolting through her. Boy, it felt good to be out from under the stress of fighting her feelings for Seth. Freeing, in fact.

Bless her precious son for showing her the way.

As Kim headed to the bathroom to brush her teeth, though, familiar doubts swamped her.

She held her breath.

You can do this, Kim.

Face the fire. Reap the reward.

A risk, for sure. But one she had to take if she was going to follow her heart and trust in Seth.

Seth rummaged around in the kitchen cupboard for his favorite cereal, thoughts of Kim dancing around in his mind, teasing him.

Man, it had felt good to hold her near. He couldn't remember being so content just to sit in quiet and listen to the sound of another person breathing. He'd really felt as if he'd been right where he belonged.

Still, he hadn't slept much last night; he was walking out onto an unstable cliff by letting himself care about Kim, and he'd had trouble getting around that truth. Doubts had crept in. Was he making a mistake by becoming so involved with Kim and Dylan?

As the long night had worn on, his thoughts had moved to the idea that had come upon him when they'd been talking about her desire to go to college. He was definitely in a position to help her with that endeavor. So, just about the time dawn had broken fully, spreading watery light into his bedroom, he'd made his decision about offering to pay her tuition.

He was excited to tell her his news.

A knock sounded on his front door.

Who would be here this early? His mom was an

early riser and baker, so maybe she was delivering some of her famous cinnamon rolls. His stomach growled at the thought. He opened the door, and to his astonishment, Kim stood on the other side. His heart rose.

"Hey," he said. "What a nice surprise." No better time than now to tell her about his own surprise. He'd never been good at hiding stuff like that.

She smiled awkwardly, then hoisted her purse over her shoulder, shifting on her feet. "Um…may I come in?"

"Sure. Everything okay?"

"I just need to talk to you."

Hmm. Talking. Not his strong suit. But he was getting better. Thanks to Kim. Still, he had the feeling something was wrong. Uneasiness spread through him.

He stepped back and gestured for her to step through the door. "You want some breakfast?"

She moved past him, shaking her head. "No, thanks. I already ate. But I could use some water."

He shut the door. "Coming right up," he said, making his way to the kitchen. "You on your way to work?"

"Um…yeah, yeah," she said, putting her purse down on his leather recliner. She then followed him into the kitchen. "I'm going there to open up." She began to chew on her bottom lip. She seemed…nervous. Edgy. Was she having second thoughts about their kiss? Funny, but he hoped not.

What was up? "Great." His voice cracked and he nearly dropped the glass he was getting from the cupboard over the dishwasher. "I was going to stop at the bank on the way in."

"Okay," she said, shoving her hands into her jeans pockets.

He filled the glass with ice, then tap water. "Listen," he said, handing the glass over. "I know how you want to go to college in Seattle."

She nodded.

"So I spent some time online last night when I got home, looking at the website for Seattle Community College."

She took a sip of water. "I've seen it. They have a great early education program at their central campus."

He forced himself to plunge onward with his news. "And, well, I've been thinking, and thought it might be nice if you were to have some help with expenses."

"Like a scholarship?"

"Kind of," he said, shrugging.

"I've actually applied for a few, but I haven't heard back yet." She chuckled. "Hope they don't look at my high school grades. I wasn't exactly into studying back then."

"But you are now, right?"

"Yes, of course. I'll have to work while I go to school, but I fully intend to study as much as possible." She slanted him a glance. "Do you know of a scholarship?"

"I do."

"Tell me about it."

"Well, the thing is, I have some money saved…"

She peered at him, her eyes narrow. "Are you offering to pay for my college?"

He nodded. "I am."

She continued staring at him, then very deliberately, it seemed, she set the water on the counter, turned her eyes down and studied the floor.

A rock landed in his gut.

When she looked back up at him, she had her mouth clamped into a thin, uncompromising line. "So let me get this straight," she said, her voice deceptively calm. Too calm. "You're offering to pay for me to go away. To college?"

"Pretty much, yes. I thought it would help you, make things easier, maybe allow you not to work so you could spend more time with Dylan."

She grabbed the glass of water and took another drink, then set the glass back on the counter with a *thunk*. "You know how much I want to be independent. Why would I be happy about you trying to take over my life?"

He grimaced. "I'm not trying to take over your life. I'm just trying to help you realize your dream. Didn't you say God would help you? Maybe he is, through me." The minute the words left his mouth, he regretted them.

She scoffed. "Egotistical of you, isn't it, thinking you're the answer to my prayers?"

Whoa. When she put it that way it did sound really bad. He opened his mouth but had no idea what to say. He'd messed this up. Royally. He could see that train coming for sure.

"I can take care of my dreams on my own, thank you very much," she said when he didn't speak. "I don't need your help."

He looked at the ceiling. He was an idiot. "I never thought you couldn't. I just thought college might happen sooner this way." Lame. He saw that now. He'd known deep down that this was the wrong way to go about things, but had forged onward, scared to death to face his feelings for her head-on, needing the familiarity of his walls. Needing to shove her away.

She swiped her face. "Maybe so, but you know how much I want to make it on my own. Right?"

"Yeah, you've told me that," he said. Acidic regret began eating away at him, burning in his gut like a flaming fastball.

She let out a quivering breath and closed her

eyes. "So you want to get rid of me that badly," she stated softly, her words coated in hurt. "Push me away like you do everybody else?"

Man, oh, man. He looked at the floor, feeling about the size of an ant. "I thought going to college in Seattle was what you wanted," he said, trying to justify what he'd done, knowing deep inside that he couldn't. Shouldn't even try.

"It is—was—but not…like this." She spun on her heel, grabbed her purse and slung it over her shoulder in rough, jerky motions. "This is all wrong. I've got to go."

Panic set in. "Kim, wait." She was slipping away from him, and he hated the chasm echoing in his chest. Even though he'd brought this on himself. "I'm sorry."

She turned around slowly. "Me, too," she said, her watery, wounded gaze hitting him hard. She pressed a hand to her mouth, then dropped it. "I refuse your offer, Seth. I will make it on my own. I don't need you."

But I need you.

He rocked back on his heels, his jaw slack, still making sense of that thought. Uncharted territory, here. He was out of his league, a minor league rookie trying to play in the majors, floundering. "I…I just wanted to help."

She shook her head slowly. "Well, you've helped

me all right. You've helped me to realize I've let myself get way too caught up in you."

Her words were like baseball-bat whacks to his heart, even though he understood them.

She drew herself up, her shoulders rigid. "Seth, I can't work for you anymore."

"Why not?" he asked. Her move made sense, though, after what he'd done.

"Because this," she said, motioning in the air between them, "isn't working for me."

He reached out, just wanting to hold her, to soothe away his stupid mistake.

She backed away toward the door.

No dice. He expected no less from a strong woman like her. He dropped his arms. "Don't go."

"I have to," she said, lifting her chin. "I've been foolish for letting my defenses down enough for you to hurt me."

"I didn't mean to hurt you," he said. But he had. Brilliant move, Graham. Really brilliant.

"Doesn't matter. The result is the same, right?"

She had him there. He'd messed this up. And now he saw that he didn't want her to walk out of his life.

How could he make her stay, though? He paced away, then swung around, his hands on his hips. "You owe me two weeks." He wasn't ready to give up yet. He'd lost this battle—been obliterated, actually. But maybe he could still win the war. At the very least he wanted a chance.

"No problem," she said stonily. "I can always use the money."

His stomach folded.

Without another word, she turned and walked out the door.

Despair jammed a knife through him, slashing his heart into ragged chunks, leaving an aching wound inside him. He didn't want to lose her.

Suddenly, the thought of being without Kim and Dylan for the rest of his life washed over him and he felt a cold chill zap down his spine. Regret drove into him, shoving the breath from his lungs.

He'd taken the easy way out. Even the seven-year-old Sharks were braver than he was. He sank down onto the couch and dropped his head into his hands, reality pressing down, hard.

Face it. He'd whiffed.

And had probably lost the best thing that had ever happened to him.

The Community Church loomed before Seth, glowing like a beacon in the misty morning coastal fog that was common in Moonlight Cove this time of year.

Needing fresh air, and something, anything, to

help soothe the wound on his heart, he'd decided to walk to work after Kim had left him alone, regretting what he'd done.

And now, here he was, having arrived at this spot in front of the church without conscious thought.

His heart burning, despair fraying the edges of his emotions, he looked up at the tall, white steeple, shooting toward the gray sky, and the colorful stained-glass windows that lined the lower wall of the sanctuary. The double wooden doors of the church stood open, inviting him in.

You can find what you need here, they seemed to say. *God listens.*

A sense of purpose overtook him. He moved forward and walked through those beckoning doors. Kim's words about how to forge a deeper, more intimate relationship with God resonated in him, like a calming, rational echo in his soul.

He needed to ask God for help. And he needed to have faith He would answer—the faith Kim had seen in Seth when he hadn't been able to see it in himself.

Stepping through the small entryway, he went directly to the sanctuary. With his eyes focused on the large crucifix holding Jesus Christ in the middle of the altar, he kept walking down the center aisle, then stopped next to the pew nearest the pulpit.

And there, he fell to his knees and began to pray, sure, this time, God would heed his call.

Because Seth believed.

He'd learned that from the woman…

The woman he loved.

The thought dawned on him quickly, like a bolt of lightning striking him right through the heart.

He loved Kim. Everything about her. She was kind, funny, warm and witty. She was a great mom, a strong person, she had a deep sense of faith he admired, and she'd raised a fantastic kid, whom Seth also loved.

It was time to kick down his walls. For good.

Thank You, God, for showing me the truth.

Now it was up to Seth to tell Kim how much he cared about her.

Would she listen?

Chapter Seventeen

An hour after she arrived at work, Kim tried to lose herself in helping a nice tourist family from Seattle pick out beginner fishing gear for their three kids.

The kids were adorable, but nothing could distract her from the hurt raging inside her. She'd been ready to risk her heart, and Seth wanted to take away her independence. He'd built the barrier so high between them, it could never be breached.

Her cheeks burned, her chest felt raw and empty. How could she have been so foolish to let her defenses fall so easily? She'd known the way Seth operated. Known how he pushed people away, and why. How could she have let herself believe he'd ever let her into his life?

Never again. She could only depend on herself and God from now on.

She rang up the sale, one eye on the hall leading to Seth's office. He was holing up again, of course. That was his M.O. *Shut down. Cut others off. Whack 'em at the knees.*

And in the heart.

He'd arrived not long ago, while she'd been helping Jasper Wendt with lures. With a cursory wave but nothing else, Seth had gone straight to his office and she hadn't seen him since. He'd made his point. Eloquently.

She had to be strong and withstand the last two weeks at work she'd promised Seth, with her heart—or what was left of it—intact. Or convince Seth's mom to come back. Whatever it took. Being here at the store every day, with him, wouldn't work. Every time she looked at him, she would be reminded of what would never be. And that would be…torture.

She needed to leave him behind, purge him from her heart. Move on. What other choice did she have?

The phone rang. She picked it up and said, "The Sports Shack, Kim speaking. How may I help you?"

"Kim, it's Benny." He sounded shook up. Frantic.

Kim pulled her eyebrows together, gripping the phone hard. "Benny, what's wrong?"

"Well, your aunt and I were out to brunch, and on the way home…" He drew in an audibly shaky breath. "…some yahoo ran a red light…and…we were in a car accident."

Fear and sharp-edged dread ricocheted through Kim. "Oh, no. Is everyone okay?"

"I'm okay, but I'm not sure about Rose. She's injured and unconscious—" His voice broke. "I think you'd better get here to the hospital."

Kim's stomach dipped, then slid down further, until it was in the vicinity of her knees. "I'll be right there." She hung up, panic rising inside her like a choking, burning tide.

Sick with dread, she ran back to Seth's office and hurriedly pushed open the door. He was working on his computer, a spreadsheet program open before him.

"Aunt Rose has been in a car accident, and I have to go to the hospital," she announced without preamble, trying to keep her voice from breaking. "Can you cover me out front?"

His head shot up, his face going ashen. He jumped to his feet. "I'll go with you."

She stepped into the office and held up a firm hand. "No, someone needs to stay here." Even though a big part of her would like to have him with her. Crazy. Hadn't she learned anything about him?

"Are you kidding me?" He shooed her back through the door. "This is an emergency. The store can wait."

"Okay. Whatever," she said, turning to hurry down the hall, her eyes burning. "I won't argue. It'd be futile, anyway."

He followed her quickly down the hall. "Yes, it would. No way do I want you to go through something like this alone."

His concern warmed up a tiny piece of cold, empty space in her heart. But most of her insides were still frozen with dread.

Almost running, they went out the front, and Seth quickly turned the sign in the window to CLOSED and locked the door behind them.

Kim hurried to her car, Seth following close behind. Fright grabbed at her, and her tummy turned over and over. What was she going to do if something happened to Aunt Rose? The horrifying thought was simply too much to bear.

Kim frantically dug in her purse for her keys, and found them at the very bottom, of course. She took them out, gripping the key chain hard, trying not to lose control and panic completely. She had to be strong for Aunt Rose.

Her hands were shaking too much to get the car key in the door lock.

Seth took them. "Here, let me. I'll drive," he said.

She nodded her assent and hopped into the front passenger seat.

Seth took off toward the only hospital in Moonlight Cove, expertly maneuvering her Honda onto the highway, probably driving too fast. Kim didn't care. All that mattered was getting to Aunt Rose. A prayer formed in Kim's heart, echoing through her like a litany, giving her a measure of control when she felt as if she had none.

Please, Lord. If You save Aunt Rose, I'll never ask anything else of You again.

Halfway there, Seth looked over when they stopped at a light. "She's going to be okay."

"I hope so," Kim choked out, her eyes burning even more. "I don't know what I'll do if I lose her."

"You're not going to lose her," he said, his voice soothing and strong. "She's as strong as an ox."

Kim's lips trembled. "She is, isn't she?"

Seth reached over and took her hand in his. "You bet she is."

Kim held on to him, drawing strength from his support. She was thankful he was here. Good or bad, she needed support.

They arrived at the hospital, parked in the Emergency Room parking lot and quickly exited the car. It had started to rain, and the gray skies and drizzle seemed somehow appropriate.

Her heart felt just as ashen.

It was hard for Kim to believe that Seth had been here not so long ago, getting the stitches still visible on his forehead. So much had happened since then. So much had changed. And now things were spinning out of control...

She hurried inside, Seth right next to her. The nurse at the front desk directed them to an E.R. waiting area where they found Benny, sitting alone in the corner, looking worse for the wear, but uninjured. His wavy gray hair was mussed, his untucked shirttail hung out on one side and a sickly pallor clung to his drawn face.

He saw Kim and stood, and she was struck by the look of sheer desolation shining from his eyes. Her stomach fell, and nausea rose. Oh, no...

Kim sobbed, and tears rolled. "Aunt Rose...is she...?" She couldn't bear to say the words. She felt Seth's hand on her back.

Benny took her hands. "No, no. She's still hanging in there."

Kim let out a shaky breath, immensely grateful Aunt Rose was still alive.

Thank you, God.

"But she does have internal injuries," Benny said, his voice low. "They're doing surgery now to figure out exactly what's damaged."

Kim hugged him, then stepped back. Her lips trembled as she wiped tears from her cheeks. "Wow. Do they think she's going to be all right?

"They're cautiously optimistic."

Kim nodded, a lump forming in her throat.

Seth stepped close and put his arm around her. "Why don't you sit down," he said, guiding her to a chair. "I'll get you some water."

She nodded, then sank into an ugly gray upholstered chair. Benny sat down beside her, sighing heavily.

"What happened?" she asked.

Benny shook his head. "Some hotshot kid in a souped-up car trying to make the light at Ocean and First T-boned us on your aunt's side, and he walked away without a scratch." He put his head in his hands. "I can't lose her now that I've just found her."

Kim stared at him, blinking. "You love her, don't you?"

"With all my heart."

"She is pretty special, isn't she?"

Benny raised his head and sat back in the chair. "After my wife died, I never thought I'd find someone like Rose. But I did find a wonderful woman, and I can't let someone as perfect as my Rose slip through my fingers."

Kim tilted her head in a nod, Benny's emotions touching her. "Were you scared to fall in love?"

Benny looked at her, his eyes questioning. "No, not at all. Why?"

The need to unburden herself overwhelmed her. "Because I'm scared to let myself love Seth."

"Yeah," he said, inclining his head to the side. "Your aunt feels the same way about love, doesn't she?"

"Must run in the family."

He chuckled under his breath. "Must. Guess I'll just have to convince her otherwise, won't I?"

"How're you going to do that?" Kim asked.

"By telling her that the thought of my life without her just won't work."

Kim stared at him. "Maybe I've been overthinking things, you know?"

He reached out and patted her hand. "I gave up over-thinking a long time ago. You miss too much in life if you let your brain rule your heart."

She gripped his hand, a rush of affection for him moving through her. "How did you get to be so smart?"

"Lots of living and lots of mistakes. Maybe you can learn from some of mine." He pointed at her. "If you love Seth, well, then, don't let him go."

Kim could barely breathe. Benny's words resonated inside her, and made her think more deeply about Seth. Yes, he'd gone about helping her with college in a way that made her angry. But he was human, too, with his own foibles and flaws, just as she was. And he'd grown up in a very dysfunctional family. Was it any wonder he'd handled things the way he had, given the examples of love that had formed him?

No, it wasn't.

She had to forgive him.

Seth returned with water and handed one paper cup to her and one to Benny.

"Thanks," she said, looking up at him, seeing what a wonderful man he was, how unselfish and kind. Clumsy at relationships, too. But that was fixable.

"Anything else I can get?" He looked to Benny. "Have you eaten? I could go get you something at the cafeteria."

"No," Benny said with a wave of his hand. "I don't think I'd be able to eat right now."

"Well, let me know what you need when you need it and I'll be happy to get it for you," Seth said, patting Benny's arm.

Seth sat down next to Kim, and a warm, cared-for feeling washed over her. He was something, all right. Really something, taking care of everyone around him.

They sat for a while in silence. Kim sipped her water, and couldn't help but turn Benny's words over and over in her brain again, examining them from every angle. Was he right? Should she grab Seth and never let him go? Could she take that risk? And was that risk worth the price she might pay?

Yes.

The waiting became interminable. Grief and despair and sadness frayed the edges of her control, and she found herself crying as she stopped at the window and looked out through her tears at the green trees dotting the hospital grounds.

A prayer rolled through her, strong and pleading.

Please, Heavenly Father. Help Rose pull through this...

Within seconds she felt strong arms turn her around and pull her close.

Seth. She wrapped her arms around him and held him tight, so, so glad he was here for her in her time of need. Because...she did need him. More than she ever thought possible.

He was her rock.

He murmured words of comfort and encouragement in her ear and rubbed her back in soothing circular motions. She melted into his strong embrace, drawing strength from him. For the first time in her life, she felt as if she were right where she belonged.

What would she do without him? She didn't want to find out.

She saw that she didn't have to do everything on her own. Suddenly, all of her doubts and fears fell away, leaving only the beautiful truth glowing in her heart.

Yes, she did love Seth, and she was sure God would want her to have the security of human love.

A calm came over her. She'd made her decision. She opened her mouth to tell Seth, right now, but the doctor came in. She could wait. But not long.

She didn't want to lose him.

That just wasn't an option any more.

"Rose is going to recover," the doctor said, taking off his glasses. "Her spleen was injured, but we repaired it. The broken ribs will take some time to heal, but she won't have any lasting effects from them."

Relief washed over Seth as Kim and Benny hugged each other in joy at the good news. He couldn't decide which one of them looked happier about Rose being okay. It had been a long, difficult wait for all of them. The news was good. Seth was glad he'd been there for them. Really glad.

"How long will she need to stay in the hospital?" Benny asked.

"A few days, so we can be sure her pain is lessened. She'll need to take it easy for a while once she goes home, but I'm sure between the three of you, you'll manage."

The three of them.

Seth liked being included in this family group.

He liked it a lot. More than he'd ever expected. With even more certainty he knew that he didn't want to lose Kim, didn't want to miss being a part of this family.

He was up for the challenge.

Was Kim?

"We'll take good care of her, Doc," Benny said. "Luckily I live right next door." He craned his head to look down the hall. "When can we see her?"

"She's in recovery right now, so it'll be at least an hour or two before she's ready for visitors."

Seth looked at Kim. She had dark circles under her eyes from her makeup smudging, and she looked dog tired, but she was still the most beautiful woman he'd ever seen. Inside and out.

She glanced at her watch. "Oh, goodness, I have to go pick up Dylan from Vacation Bible School at the beach."

"I'll go get him," Seth said.

"Why don't you both go," Benny said. "You look like you could use the break. I'll wait here."

Kim tapped her lip with a finger.

Benny touched her shoulder. "Go. The doc said it'll be a few hours, anyway. You'll be back in plenty of time."

"Good idea, Benny," Seth said. Kim needed a breather. "Besides, we're going to have to tell

Dylan his auntie has been in an accident, and I'd like to be there when you tell him."

Kim smiled softly at him, her eyes holding on his. "That's sweet." She sucked in a breath, then turned to Benny. "Okay. Don't you worry, though. We'll be right back."

"I'll be here when you return, holding down the fort."

Seth put his hand on the small of Kim's back and guided her down the hall to the elevator, and then to the car. She seemed small and fragile to him, and he wanted nothing more than to take her in his arms and soothe away her worries.

He couldn't push her away any more. No way. He loved her. Now more than ever.

They reached her car. "You want me to drive again?" he asked.

"I think you better. I'm still feeling shaky."

Once they were on their way to nearby Moonlight Cove beach, Seth darted a glance over at Kim. She was staring right at him, her brown eyes probing.

His stomach flip-flopped. "What's up?"

"I have to say something."

Ominous words. "Okay," he said more calmly than he felt.

She paused, laughing without humor under her breath. "I thought this would be easier."

He rubbed his jaw. Great. She was going to tell

him to get lost. Drop the ax again. He wanted to stop the car and jump out and avoid the pain he saw coming, to shut down, run away. Fortify his walls. Protect his heart.

His natural reaction.

But he wouldn't take off. Not this time. He was done running, done letting his old fears drive his choices. Done shutting her out.

Kim had taught him how to open up.

How to have faith.

"Hold on, we're almost there." He didn't want to be driving for this conversation, for the sake of anyone else on the road. He pulled into the beach parking lot and wheeled the nimble car into a spot. He put the gear in Park and cut the engine, his heart galloping.

Looking at the amazing woman before him, he knew what he had to do. He had to fight for her, just as he fought the ocean the day he'd saved her. Time to lay it on the line.

Swing, baby, swing. Don't worry if you strike out. Just play ball.

She opened her mouth to speak, but he held up a hand and stopped her. "Before you say anything, I need to talk."

Blinking, she nodded.

He took a deep breath and forged ahead. "I met you and Dylan, and I knew you two were special right off. And that scared me, a lot."

"I know," she said, her lips trembling. "It scared me, too."

They were alike that way. "I fought falling for you, but I've seen what a wonderful woman you are. And I don't want to fight my feelings anymore. Actually, I can't fight my feelings anymore." He took her hand. "I love you, Kim Hampton. And I love your son, too."

Her mouth formed a surprised "O."

A long second later, his declaration seemed to sink in. A joyful smile lit up her face. She threw her arms around his neck and hugged him tight. "I love you, too," she whispered. "That's what I wanted to tell you."

Elation zigzagged through him, joy trailing in its wake. "What took you so long?" he asked, his voice husky. "You kept me hanging."

She pulled back. "I was so, so scared, too." She gave him a shaky yet rueful smile. "And I was a little angry after we talked this morning. I thought you were pushing me away."

Regret ate through him. "I'm sorry I did that," he said. "I wasn't thinking clearly."

"I'll forgive you just this once," she said, still smiling, obviously teasing.

He grinned, loving this woman more and more. "I'm glad," he stated, touching her cheek, feeling her silky skin against his fingertips. Gorgeous. Perfect. "And I'm not scared anymore."

"Why not?" she asked, her words a caress, her brown eyes suddenly misty.

"Because almost losing you was the scariest thing I've ever faced." He kissed her. "But this..." He kissed her again. "This is just plain right."

With love shining from her eyes, she said, "I agree, Mr. Graham. Wholeheartedly."

He leaned in for another kiss, but a knock on the car's window stopped him.

"Hold that thought," he said to Kim, then rolled down the window. Dylan stood waiting in denim shorts, a hooded sweatshirt and his Sharks baseball cap. He had sand sticking to him from head to toe and his nose looked a bit sunburned.

"Hey, Coach." Flashing his gap-toothed grin, he waved. "What're you doing here?"

"Picking you up." Seth looked at Kim, smiling tenderly. Man, he loved this woman and her son. "We should fill him in."

She nodded, her face lighting up. "Tell him about us first. Then we'll tell him about Rose," she whispered. "I'm so glad she's going to be okay."

Seth opened the door and stood as Kim got out of her side and came over to stand beside him and Dylan. "We have some news for you," she said, her voice as bright as the sun that was beginning to peek through the clouds.

Seth's heart filled with light.

Dylan nodded, his eyes wide. "'Kay."

Seth took a hold of Kim's hand. "Your mom and I...well, we love each other."

"Yeah." Dylan shrugged. "I know."

Seth hoisted up both his eyebrows. "How did you know?"

"Because in my prayers last night I asked God to make you guys love each other."

Impressed and astounded that a seven-year-old already knew what had taken him twenty-eight years to learn, Seth looked at Kim, his eyebrows raised high, his chin lowered slightly as if to say, "Can you believe this kid?"

She shrugged, obviously getting his nonverbal message loud and clear. Her pretty eyes sparkled. "Hey, what can I say? I told you God was a pretty dependable guy."

"Yes, you did." With happiness overflowing, he reached out, took her small hand in his and drew her near. "Thankfully, I listened," he said, pulling his arm around her slim shoulders.

Dylan watched them intently for a few seconds. "So when are you guys gonna get all mushy, like they do on TV?"

"Mushy?" Seth reached out, snatched the hat from Dylan's head and plopped it on his own. "I'll show you mushy." With a hoot, he grabbed Dylan and swung him up in the air, bringing him down into his arms.

Dylan squealed.

Seth held him tight with one arm, his heart expanding, and opened his other arm toward Kim. With a glowing smile, she stepped into his embrace, completing the circle.

Completing him.

A deep, abiding contentment flooded through him, filling up all of his empty spaces. No doubt about it, this amazing family had rescued him just when he'd needed saving the most.

That's what happened when a guy had faith.

Thank You, God, for answering my prayers.

Epilogue

"Keep your eye on the ball, Dylan, and swing when the ball's in the zone," Seth called, clapping. "You've got this."

Dylan gave Seth a quick nod, then got back into position in the batter's box, zeroing in on the pitcher.

Kim looked at Seth sitting next to her in the Moonlight Cove Elementary School baseball field bleachers, her heart swelling with love, happiness flowing through her like a warm, comforting tide.

Who would have guessed when Seth had rescued her from the ocean that fateful day on the beach over a month ago that she would now be sitting next to the most wonderful man in the world. And that he'd love her. And that they'd be here together on this beautiful, cloudless summer day, looking more and more like a family.

God had truly blessed her by bringing Seth into her life.

A female voice rang out from Kim's right. "Send it, Dyl. Clear to the beach."

Kim smiled and slanted a glance at Aunt Rose.

Fortunately, Rose was feeling good enough to come to the game, her first major outing since the car accident two weeks ago. She still tired easily but was well on the way to a total recovery.

Benny had been by her side during the whole process and had come to the game with them, hovering over Rose like a man in love. Rose had been cagey about her feelings for her attentive neighbor, but Kim saw the way she looked at Benny. Kim suspected there was going to be a wedding in Rose and Benny's future.

And in hers? Definitely. Soon, if she had her way.

Kim reached out and took Seth's hand in hers. He smiled at her, his eyes crinkling at the corners and, as usual, her heart melted. "Trying to distract me from the action on the field?" he asked, his tone teasing.

She returned his smile and squeezed his hand, giving a little shrug. "I can't help it. And you're the one distracting me."

"Well, then in that case, let's do it right," he

said, putting his well-muscled arm around her shoulders, squeezing her up against his side.

She snuggled close, breathing in his scent, her head resting on his shoulder for a brief moment. No doubt about it—she was one happy woman. No, make that ecstatic. She saw nothing but good things in her future with Seth.

Since that pivotal day in the hospital when she'd realized how much she needed Seth, she'd really embraced the notion that she didn't have to do everything on her own. That realization, in turn, had helped her to accept the blessing of having Aunt Rose and Seth around to help her if need be. So her plans for moving to Seattle had been put on hold.

However, one of Seth's old Mariners teammates had approached Seth about working together on opening a second Sports Shack store in Seattle in the near future, and Seth was seriously thinking about accepting the offer. If he did, they'd decided that Kim and Dylan would go with him and she'd start early education classes as soon as possible.

The hint of a wedding before the move had thrilled Kim—and Dylan, too. Add to that the exciting news that Seth's younger brother, Ian, wanted to move to Moonlight Cove to run The Sports Shack if Kim and Seth did indeed move to Seattle, and life was looking good.

All kinds of dreams seemed to be coming true these days.

Refocusing on the game, she looked toward Dylan, hoping he got on base. It was the bottom of the last inning, and the score was tied zip, zip. He'd struck out the last time he'd batted, and she was sure he needed the confidence booster of a good, clean hit that would help win the game for the Sharks.

He wanted to be just like Seth.

Smart kid.

The pitcher wound up, and Kim focused on Dylan, holding her breath. The pitcher threw the ball…and…high. Way high. Dylan swung…and missed.

Kim bit her lip.

"No problem," Seth immediately called. "You've got this, Dyl. Keep your eye on the ball, and you'll connect."

Dylan put himself back into the batter's box and honed in on the pitcher again. The ball left the pitcher's hands…and *crack!* It went sailing across the field, way past the outfielders, almost to the evergreen trees edging the field.

Wow!

Dylan ran toward first—boy, he was fast—and Kim got to her feet, cheering. "Go, Dyl, go!"

The boys in the outfield scrambled for the ball.

His arms pumping, Dylan rounded the corner and headed toward second. The center fielder found the ball and wound up to throw…

Dylan hit third in a streak of blue and white… and then put on the afterburners and cruised home, just as the pitcher snagged the ball. Too late.

The Sharks had won!

The crowd went wild as Dylan pulled up in front of the backstop, his face split into a huge grin. Kim jumped and whooped along with everybody else, pride spreading through her like warm molasses.

Dylan took off his batting helmet and ran to the Sharks' bench, high-fiving down the line of his jubilant teammates.

Still grinning, he headed over to Kim, Seth, Benny and Rose, his hands in the air. "I did it!" he crowed. "I did it!"

"Good for you," Seth said, squeezing Dylan's narrow shoulder, his voice rife with obvious pride. "Your first homer."

"Way to go," Kim replied, hugging Dylan tight. She looked up and her gaze connected with Seth's across the few feet that separated them.

He stared right at her, his blue eyes warm with love.

Amazing.

Seth stepped forward and wrapped his arms

around her and Dylan, encircling them in his strong, steady embrace. Joy unfurled inside of her, bright and wonderful.

Dylan had won his game, and she'd won at love.

What more could she ask for?

* * * * *

Dear Reader,

Welcome to Moonlight Cove! I'm thrilled you are reading about this heartwarming community on the Washington coast, especially since it was based on a small coastal Oregon town I spent a lot of time in while I was growing up, vacationing at my aunt's oceanfront cabin. The Pacific Northwest coast is a beautiful place, and a perfect setting for a romance. What better spot to have two stubborn people fall in love, with the gorgeous Pacific Ocean and stunning coastline as the backdrop?

I had a lot of fun creating the characters who live in Moonlight Cove, and I am planning other books set in the quaint town, featuring Main Street business owners and their families. Stay tuned.

I am a huge dog lover, and based Cleo on my own standard poodle, Jade. Look for Cleo in a book in the future, as well as Aunt Rose and Benny, and perhaps Kim's cousin, Grant. Of course, heartwarming romance will always be the true star in my stories. I really enjoy writing about people who never think they will fall in love, but inevitably do. Happy endings always make my day.

I love to hear from my readers; it is gratifying

to know that people actually spend time with the characters I have lovingly created. Feel free to contact me via email at: lissa@lissamanley.com, or via Steeple Hill Books.

Blessings,

Lissa Manley

QUESTIONS FOR DISCUSSION

1. Kim had an impulsive nature that had landed her in trouble in the past, and she felt guilty for her role in causing Seth's injury. Was her guilt justified? Was she irresponsible by going in the ocean? How could she have handled the situation differently?

2. Seth rescued Kim without thinking of the danger to himself. Was this heroic or foolish? What does the answer say about his character?

3. Seth was uncomfortable being called a hero and wanted to downplay his actions. Discuss why.

4. Seth felt like emotional connections caused pain, and he limited getting attached to others—and God—to protect himself. Discuss why some people close themselves off after emotional trauma and others don't.

5. Seth grew up in a dysfunctional family and blamed his parents' constant fighting for many of the problems in his life. Was this fair? Why or why not?

6. Kim was abandoned by her father and her ex-husband, and she felt she must build walls to protect herself from depending on anyone. Yet she was willing to depend on her aunt Rose and God. Discuss why.

7. As a child, Seth prayed to God to make his parents stop fighting, and his prayers didn't work, hurting his faith in God. Was this understandable, or should he have given God another chance?

8. Kim wanted to limit contact between Seth and her son, Dylan, to protect Dylan from getting hurt. Was this reasonable? Or selfish? Were her protective instincts justified?

9. Do you agree with Kim's belief that Seth was willing to connect with the boys on the baseball team because he felt less threatened by kids than by adults?

10. Kim was angry that Seth agreed to coach the baseball team without asking her first. Was he wrong to agree without consulting her, or did his desire to not disappoint Dylan justify his actions? Did Kim overreact?

11. Kim told Seth that he needed to have faith to find faith, and to deepen his connection with God. How has this idea worked in your life?

12. Seth decided to offer to pay for Kim's college tuition. Why did he do this? Were his actions true to his character?

13. Aunt Rose ended up changing her mind about Seth. In your opinion, did Seth earn her trust?

14. Dylan trusted Seth and ended up showing Kim that she should trust Seth, too. Discuss how a child in your life has taught you an important lesson and why children are sometimes able to see to the heart of the matter more easily than adults.

LARGER-PRINT BOOKS!

**GET 2 FREE
LARGER-PRINT NOVELS
PLUS 2 FREE
MYSTERY GIFTS**

Larger-print novels are now available...

Love Inspired ® SUSPENSE

RIVETING INSPIRATIONAL ROMANCE

Watch for our series of edge-
of-your-seat suspense novels.
These contemporary tales
of intrigue and romance
feature Christian characters
facing challenges to their faith...
and their lives!

AVAILABLE IN REGULAR
& LARGER-PRINT FORMATS

For exciting stories that reflect traditional values,
visit:
www.ReaderService.com